plonk goes the weasel

by Joan Del Monte

Cover design by Tim Brady, www.writeuptheroad.com

ISBN 0-7414-1778-2

Published by:

PUBLISHING.COM

519 West Lancaster Avenue
Haverford, PA 19041-1413
Info@buybooksontheweb.com
www.buybooksontheweb.com
Toll-free (877) BUY BOOK
Local Phone (610) 520-2500
Fax (610) 519-0261

Printed in the United States of America

Printed on Recycled Paper

Published November 2003

Dedication

To St. Rita of the Impossible

plonk goes the weasel

Chapter One

The first check that bounced in Plonktown was Henry Richard's.

Henry picked up the check from the film company at his post office box at 11:45 on a Saturday morning in late October. The post office still had the little brass doors with windows on each compartment, and he saw the letter through the glass. He ripped open the envelope as soon as he saw it. He was a reasonable man and reason told him the check would be coming, yet his first impulse was to do a little victory sidestep right there in the post office vestibule.

He started back across the plaza to the furniture store to tell Sally right away; she worried about the damn money. But he bent down to pick up a penny off the sidewalk, looking over his shoulder left and right to make sure nobody saw. His mother always used to say finding a penny was good luck. It meant money was coming. His mother was eleven when she came over from Italy, and she also still ate lentils on New Year's Eve because she believed the coin shape of the lentils meant money in the coming year.

Henry got rid of the lentils, but he could never pass up a penny.

This year the plaza looked different, since the film company took out all the TV antennas and put a coat of white paint on everything to make it look like it was the 1950's. Broxton Films had used the town the whole spring and summer making their TV pilot. Hell, the movie house even took down its marquee, which was art deco zigzags, and put one up in neon. Henry thought the downtown looked nice. Clean.

Henry glanced at his watch. Instead of going back to the store, he'd turn right on the sidewalk and go to the bank before they closed at noon. That way he could tell Sally he had started the paperwork to get the second trust deed off the real estate at the store.

The Plonktown bank was a one story tan brick fortress, an anomaly among the tall wood Victorians that surrounded the plaza. The marble floor was wet with smears of mud

1

from the busy Saturday morning. For all the people milling around trying to beat the noon closing, the Plonktown bank gave an immediate impression of wood—polished wood teller counters with glass windows, wood tables holding deposit slips, much of it wood from the redwoods dripping outside in the Northern California pale grey midday. The smell of wet wool rose from coats and scarves and mingled with the gas smell coming from the cars prowling the plaza perimeter outside looking for parking. All the wood chairs were occupied, and Henry breezed past everybody, dropping the check directly on the desk of Eric Linden, the bank manager.

"Just got it," Henry crowed. "That's the check for the furniture the film company rented from me. So I can pay you now."

"Oh." Eric picked up the check, glancing away from the heavyset man he was talking to. "Well, that's fine, just fine."

"So there's the payment. How long will it take you for the paperwork to take the second off my store?"

"Well now, Henry, the bank requires a cashier's check in payment before we start the paperwork--"

"Oh come on, Eric, you know it's good. Call up and verify the check if you have to. You still have time before you close--"

"Hey fella, you know, you're interrupting." The heavyset man straightened up.

"That's not our procedure; with real estate loans we have to be careful."

"But you can do it, can't you?" Henry asked. "Look, Eric, Sally had a fit when I put that second trust deed against the store's real estate."

"Henry, now you can see I've got somebody here at my desk--"

"Yeah, you mind?" the heavy man rumbled. "I mean, we're doing something here."

"I love Sally, God knows, but she's not a businesswoman, doesn't understand how to use debt. Well, she's an artist, of course. And you know I had to take out that second, Eric, because Humboldt County Building and

Safety was making noise about the crew filming in the store." Henry put up a hand to stop the man's protests.

"It's not going to make any difference if I start the paperwork today or Monday." Eric stapled the check to a large file folder.

"And then Building and Safety said they were going to shut me down unless I put in new electrical, even circuit breakers, for all the filming they were doing."

"And this is not the exact amount." Eric said before he closed the file.

"Yeah, I took a little extra when Herb Boland, that director, signed the contract for renting the furniture from me for the pilot. But now I got the check I want to tell Sally I paid off the loan and the paperwork is started to get it off the property. The rest of it's in my account here. Just get the paperwork going, will you?"

Eric sighed. "Okay, I'll call the bank down in Los Angeles and put a hold on the funds."

"Jesus," the heavyset man threw his hands widespread, palms up. "What is this? I mean, I'm sitting here."

"Great." Henry started to punch Eric in the arm, said "Sorry," to the man glaring at him from the other side of Eric's desk, and left.

He started across the town square, which locals called the plaza, in a rapid scoot, watching the frantic hops of the pigeons on the two walks that formed a cracked concrete X bisecting the plaza. Pigeons were probably mad because they missed the statue of Josiah Plonk, which usually stood in the small round park at the apex of the X. Now a large wooden sign in the same place said in nine-inch letters, "Broxton Films" and "A Zoltan Diesel Corporation."

"The statue's coming back!" he called out to two children. They eyed him and edged away.

Henry looked at the grass. People had started cutting across the grassy circle where the statue used to be; there was the beginning of a footpath. Now, wasn't that just the way. People wouldn't take the three or four extra steps to go around.

And he didn't like the statue of Josiah enough to understand all the fuss about moving it. Herb Boland said they'd pay to put Josiah back right after they finished shooting. Like Henry told the town council, sometimes things have to change. Henry couldn't for the life of him see why people got off on these damned tangents.

Henry sniffed the wet air as he headed toward the line of two story commercial buildings on the north side of the plaza. In the fall the stores around the plaza displayed flannel sheets and heaters and tools for building projects, and there was a precarious prosperity because of the carpentry finish work going on inside many of the houses. The small group of Humboldt County craftsmen was frantically weaving or blowing glass or turning out wood toys and redwood kitsch for the Christmas fairs which provided much of its yearly income. Because of Humboldt State University, the plaza sometimes seemed a throwback to the sixties, as men with single back braids and opaque stares congregated in the park opposite the co-op market. And then the buyers who came up to buy large quantities of Humboldt County pot in October drove their Volvos back south on Hwy 101, leaving their money to oil the Plonktown economy for another winter.

On the north side of the plaza, Henry cut across Bart Poway's gas station—something he absolutely never did, because Bart would have a fit. He didn't see Bart, but the station looked weird, because Bart had pulled out the regular gas pumps and his Standard station sign and put in outdated 1950's ones for the TV pilot.

Suddenly Bart slid out from under a car on a roller, narrowly missing Henry's foot, picked up his pliers off the ground and jammed them in his overall pocket.

"Saw your feet." he said. "Gotta watch my tools. Used to be you could stand in the plaza and say 'I forgot my hammer' and five guys would lend you one. With these damn film people here, you got the town council yelling my station should keep open a public pisser, and you can bet everybody heads for it picks up something belongs to me."

"Just got my check," Henry grinned. "Took it right to the bank."

4

"Jesus, you think mine is in? I sat at my computer last night. My income this year is way down. People didn't get their cars worked on because you couldn't drive around the plaza and besides, they were too busy gawking at the film guys."

"All the stores are down. People couldn't park because of those big movie trucks, but it doesn't matter now, with the checks in."

"Damn, look at that, the bank's closed." Bart stood up to look across the plaza. Bart had a barrel chest which had slipped to his waistline. He had to move carefully sliding from under the car. "And they won't open for me. I went to the hardware store Thursday, same damn hardware store I been doing business at for thirteen years, and they asked me for two pieces of I.D. for my check. Me!"

"It's for the insurance company; they make you get I.D. for everybody's checks. We're getting a lot of tourists now at the furniture store with all the activity." Henry shivered in the first chill spatter of rain blowing in off the Bottoms. He should have worn a coat. He hadn't planned on being out of the store so long.

"How you feel about all this depends whether you were one of the people got to work on that damn TV show or not." Bart wiped his hands. "I was for bringing in the film crew, but I'm glad to see them go. I think when this money runs out we're gonna see some real fights in this town between guys got money and guys didn't."

"The extra money helps the businesses in town; people are going to spend these checks--"

"But the people who used to make money, the people who own businesses, aren't. And the people who got some kind of TV role made big bucks."

"Bart—"

"I got two gas jockeys quit me flat right in the middle of all this just to go tote stuff for the film guys, that was some big thrill. I tell you, when them guys come back looking for work, I'm gonna say, where was you this spring when I was going crazy? I can't walk away from my job when I feel like it, why's it coming to them?"

"Bart, I want to tell Sally the check came in. I don't like to leave her alone in the store so long. I just meant to go to the post office--"

"And they parked two of those big movie trucks in the plaza and took up all the parking. And the town had to pay to move Josiah."

Henry rolled his eyes. "Which the film company will pay us back for. We've been over this and over it. You'd think we were going to melt the damn statue down instead of storing it."

"I don't think we should've moved the statue. The thing's been here since the thirties. Man founds a town, you should leave his statue alone. I think we should have said, 'This is it, this is the way we look, take it or leave it."

"So they'd have gone to another town, because that spot in the plaza was the only place they could put the drive-in restaurant set. And we all wanted to be in the pilot. It was fun, besides the money."

"Well, we better keep some of that money until the TV company puts everything back." Bart cleared his throat and spat on the ground. "I let them hook into my electricity at the gas station, because they were filming right there on the plaza. Of course, Boland said that would be no problem; all I do is forward the bill."

"Right. That's what I did about the furniture they rented from me."

"Where the hell is Boland?"

"He had to go down to Los Angeles to straighten out a few things with the producer, that Zoltan Diesel."

"Yeah, but where's the crew?"

"Bart, come on, what's wrong with you? They said they might have to come back to do a final polish. The merchants thought we could have a wrap party for them."

"A wrap party? We're talking like them now?"

"Bart, I know you're upset, but when you start talking to me like that, that just doesn't make it." Henry put his hands on his hips. He had small white hands, his fingernails scrupulously clean.

"Okay, I apologize."

6

"Yeah, but it'll happen again, you can't resist. You've been down on these film people all the time lately."

"What's all the yelling?" Sally was at the door of the furniture store. "And why don't you have a coat on, Henry, it's raining."

"Bart's starting in about Josiah's statue."

"I agree with him."

"That's because you picked up all this stuff in art school about how sculpture is site specific. So now you think it's a crime to move it."

"See what's wrong: this town doesn't look this way." Sally was tall and willowy and she waved a graceful arm to take in the plaza. "We're a real lumbering town, with redwood houses. We have a particular look and it's not the way they've made us look."

"Well, we've got their money. I was coming to tell you we just got the check from the film company."

"Oh honey, thank God." Sally threw her arms around Henry's neck. She stood a good half a head taller than he did.

"It was a dumb idea to begin with to put that trust deed on your store," Bart said.

"Bart, you're getting to be a pain in the ass on this subject," Henry said.

"All right, okay. So now my friends are telling me to shut up."

Henry knew if he didn't stop the discussion right now he was going to have an argument on his hands instead of a celebration.

"Hey," he looked over to the south side of the plaza. "Eric's coming over from the bank to tell Sally himself. Now, that's nice of him."

Eric Linden crossed the plaza with long purposeful steps. Linden always had an unhappy banker's expression, but now he looked like he was really about to make ugly noises. Henry figured he was mad because he had to stay after the bank closed at noon so he could call Los Angeles.

"I told her the news," Henry said. "About what came in the mail."

7

"You didn't tell her all of it." Linden said. "Your check? The one from the film company?"

"Yeah, what?"

"It just bounced."

Chapter Two

Zoltan Diesel had his offices in one of the prewar two story stucco Spanish mansions that lined Beverly Blvd. in Los Angeles, each embracing its own parking courtyard with two circling arms of stucco half-walls. Diesel's courtyard had orange paver tiles and his parking space had a low framed tile displaying a white Rolls, which reflected the one that Diesel parked there. The building was painted a pale apricot and beyond the courtyard a seven foot high intricate wrought iron gate displayed the entwined initials ZD, and opened to a cream colored interior tile stairway which swept up to the second floor and a seated receptionist.

The owner of this manicured hacienda was in his late thirties, with a face made rounder by thinning hair which he parted on the right. He had fresh and boyish skin, which somehow looked peculiar. The moustache was meant to be dashing and take attention away from the spotty hairline. He was wearing a short sleeved shirt tucked into gray cord slacks which displayed a flat stomach, Adidas with no socks, and he was speaking on the phone while Herb Boland fidgeted in a chair in front of his desk.

Boland's agent had said, "Watch him every single minute. He's not called Diesel the Weasel in the industry for nothing."

"Are you kidding?" Herb had said. "After all the scuzzy people I worked with--"

"I once saw Diesel walk into a room full of gray flannel suits," the agent said, "and put his feet up on the conference table with those damn sneakers with no socks. The suits just gaped and Diesel took over right from the git."

Boland compressed his lips. This conversation was not going to be controlled by Diesel. He was going to give Diesel a piece of his mind.

"—We'll put it in as a condition of sale," Diesel said on the phone, gesturing with his free hand, "The parent company has to tell their retirees to pick up the entire cost of their medical insurance or they can go get insurance on their own."

Diesel listened briefly and winked at Boland. "Owen," he interrupted the person on the phone, "The retirees aren't vested in their medical benefits; I read the contract. Once we own the business there won't be any money to pay for their medical. We're taking over the management of their pension benefits because I want those, but as to the medical, it's the end of the free ride."

He hung up and grinned at Boland. "I usually wind up not one of their favorite people on the planet."

Boland watched Diesel warily. He had been sitting in Diesel's posh reception room for a half hour. Then he had waited in front of Diesel's desk for another twenty minutes while Diesel dealt with his phone conversation. Diesel had continued the Spanish theme inside his office, with deep window embrasures and flat white walls displaying plein air paintings of Carmel and Big Sur, and framed photos of Diesel with various luminaries. Overhead, can lights provided illumination. Diesel's desk was set on a dais in front of Boland, the desktop a polished rectangle of glass large enough to seat eight. The chair Boland sat in reflected Diesel's enthusiasm for Charles Eames and was difficult to get out of; therefore Boland tried not to slump.

Boland scratched his calf. He was wearing blue jeans, a white tee shirt lettered in red, 'Humboldt Crabs Baseball Team' and gum-soled boots which he had bought in Plonktown. Although he was six inches taller than Diesel, he lost some of the height because his shoulders were turning inward and downward farther each year. He picked up a cigarette lighter embedded in polished agate off Diesel's desk and ran his long fingers over the agate until he realized he was leaving fingerprints. Then he set it hastily back on the desk top, where it clanged.

"Zoltan, look, we made promises to people, you got me in the middle of this thing," Boland said.

"I don't think the residents should hold their breath waiting to be paid." Zoltan Diesel considered his fingernails. "They're behind a long line, including the Screen Actors Guild, which we owe $48,000 on behalf of a couple of members."

10

"But, Zoltan, you could pay them. You have money."
Herb's sweeping arm took in the hacienda.

"Now that's exactly it," Diesel's hand smacked the desk
with a loud crack and Herb started. "There are people who
think because I have money, that means other people don't
have money, sort of as if there's a finite amount of money in
the world and if I have more, why that means somebody else
has less. The usual candidates are families with children. But
I'll tell you something interesting, Herb," Diesel leaned
forward, "They have asked, they have done surveys and
asked the families. And the families don't want to change the
system. They want to stay in the system, but just do better,
more like me."

"Wait a minute, Zoltan; I lived with these people in
Plonktown for six months. This is not like being a goddam
corporate raider; it's not like taking over a company and
stealing some old guy's pension."

"Oh come on, there's no reason for looking so dejected.
Nobody is going to blame you, Herb. When money dries up,
it's the same as when mergers are financed by heavy
borrowing. The bottom line is, the debt is repaid by reducing
overhead." Diesel tilted back in his chair.

"So somebody gets screwed."

"True, but it's an impersonal screw."

"What the hell does that mean?"

"Herb, it means they won't even know who to be mad
at." Diesel gestured at a computer on the side desk. "You
know, I'm writing a book on the deal as an art form."

"Great," Boland muttered, "Why me? Why do I always
get guys who think they can write because maybe they wrote
a letter home to mommy from summer camp?"

"What I'm explaining to you, Herb, is what it sometimes
takes to put a deal together." Diesel had assumed what
Boland took to be his professional expression. "I'd suggest
you listen, because you can't perform creatively unless
you've got financial backing. In other words, no money, no
film."

"But Zoltan, these people, I feel I know them, they
already got their checks."

"And two million dollars of our promised financing dried up because of the stock market crash," said Diesel, "Which is not our fault. I've explained that to you."

"Zoltan, the people up there are holding bad checks. They could pursue us legally."

"If they're calling you, Herb, explain to them what the merchants and extras up there have got to understand," Diesel's voice was calm, "is that if they tie us up legally the film can't earn anything and if the film doesn't earn anything, they don't get paid at all."

"We can't just not pay them, we signed contracts."

"I've sent their City Attorney a contract to sign stating all creditors will be paid with any net revenue the pilot might earn. He certainly isn't the sharpest lawyer in California." Diesel leaned back and prodded a legal document on his desk with his shoe, "One of those lawyers that believes the value of an argument increases with more pages. His letters run longer than my contracts. But no money means no money, even in Northern California."

"Yeah, but I'm the guy who made these promises."

"You are getting in the way of this project, Herb." Diesel sighed and clasped his hands. "Do you want to alienate what's left of our backers? You know that's going to happen if you insist on continuing to talk lawsuit."

Boland hesitated. "I've been working twenty hours a day to produce that pilot." He laced his long fingers and turned his palms up to crack his knuckles. "When I finished my last TV series I swore I'd never do it again, because I was so damn tired. But I forgot how much fun it is. I forgot how good it feels when the creative juices are flowing, meeting with the casting director, arguing with the network—but they're good arguments, arguments with people I respect."

"That is exactly what I've convinced the people who are putting up the money." Diesel said. "They have their own businesses; they're certainly not seeking legal hassles. Herb, they believe they are buying into a creative act."

"This pilot was my brainchild, Zoltan. I mean, these characters started out in my head, right? And now I see them,

12

they're played by real actors; people are discussing what the characters would or wouldn't do just as if they existed." Railroad tracks etched themselves above the bridge of Boland's largish nose.

"Herb, nobody is questioning that you're a highly gifted person. You have a thousand ideas, and some of them are worthy of Fellini."

"See, it's I'm alive in a different way when I write—I notice things around me, I notice people more, I percolate. I even dream more vividly, not about the script, just in general." Herb adjusted his butt in the chair. "And I get these ideas. Why do the ideas come at 4 A.M.? And you know I have to get out of bed and write them down, or the ideas are gone in the morning, just like a dream. Like you can remember you had a dream, but you can't remember it."

"Your touch can certainly be seen in the pilot, Herb."

"And now you start screwing around with the money. I was sitting in the middle, moving the writers from one scene to another, controlling it all." Boland's arms windmilled. "And it felt so good! I don't see why it has to end on this sour note."

"I have just finished saying we all got different things out of this pilot, you included, Herb." Diesel spoke softly, "And money wasn't necessarily the thing we got. Now you can understand that."

"But it's not much money. We could pay these people, Zoltan, and I do think they should be paid." Herb put a hand on the glass desktop.

"Do you feel strongly enough to pay their money out of your end?" Diesel's benign expression did not change but his eyes were appraising.

"No." Boland admitted.

"Well, then." Diesel stood up and walked around the huge desk to put his arm on Boland's shoulder. "Take a few days off, Herb, let me handle the network rights," he said. "Go to the desert, maybe, relax a little. Forget about Plonktown, you have to think about what's important."

"Such as?"

13

"You never exercise, Herb," Diesel poked Boland gently in the ribs. "You know that new health club, The Sporting Life, opened on Sepulveda? I just joined. They have everything, indoor and outdoor pool, saunas, everything. Look, let me take you as my guest next Thursday. You can bring Avery Ford. I may have something coming up for him in a western. You'll work out, maybe have a sauna. Pick up an application, why don't you join?"

"Kind of pricey." Boland removed his hand from Diesel's desk, leaving a large smudge.

"Well, nothing's for certain," Diesel walked Boland toward the arched walnut door, "but the studio was talking that if we brought in the pilot up North at budget there'd be a nice bonus."

"Really?" Boland's back straightened. "Zoltan, how much are we looking at? You know, things have been kind of tight for me lately." He turned back toward the office.

"No amount mentioned yet, but you know I'm on them. Remember, I said no promises."

"Well, if we could swing that bonus," Boland blinked, his eyes focused on the middle distance, "That'd make a lot of things possible. I have some really great ideas, I saw this place would make a marvelous set, it's down on Venice Beach, really period thirties."

"You betcha." Diesel tapped Boland on the back with a closed fist, guided his elbow, and turned him back toward the door. Diesel waved, and then gently closed the door behind Boland.

Diesel walked to the credenza and poured himself a cognac. He sighed contentedly and crossed his feet on the polished glass, frowned at the smudge, opened the wooden shutters, and watched the lights going on in the hills north of Wilshire Blvd. There was a light gray evening mist coming up, and the lights twinkled.

It really is a lovely evening. Worked like silk, he mused, and took a luxurious sip. Boland is unhappy, but Boland will calm down. It was always effective to use somebody between himself and the investors in a deal and it had been an inspired idea to use a creative person like Boland between himself and the townspeople on this pilot. Boland was full of enthusiasm, and for the price of a few well placed rumors about film roles and tourists, they'd brought in the pilot right on budget.

Pie in the sky always works, he mused. The easiest and most profitable deal he'd had in years.

Chapter Three

Plonktown, California was founded by lumberman Josiah Plonk in 1877 on the tidal plain of Humboldt Bay, about halfway between San Francisco and the Oregon border. It was a dozen miles north of Eureka, California, the county seat. Plonktown and Eureka fought a bitter election in 1900 to be county seat and Plonktown won the election, but was disqualified when Eureka boosters proved there were 62 votes cast by Plonktown residents although there were only 60 registered voters. The county seat election was a hundred years ago. Neither city had forgotten.

The mountains, thick with redwoods, snag the fog and hold it to the east of town, where Humboldt State University is located on land given to the state because it was so mountainous it was considered unbuildable. Therefore, from any part of town except the flat flood plain called the Bottoms, the residents enjoy a view of the sweep of Humboldt Bay. When they can see it through the fog.

The coastal fog is a primary fact of life in Humboldt County. During World War II runways and barracks were built for a Navy airport called the Landing Aids Experiment Station, and important strategic research in fog dispersal was carried out in preparation for the bombing of Germany. This airport became the Humboldt Airport. It is a local joke that a builder from Southern California built a shopping mall which he called Bay View.

The fog psychologically forms the residents. Wrapped in that fog, like soft cotton batting, they come to consider themselves isolated from the world. Humboldt has a long tradition of ignoring federal authority. During Prohibition the abundant Humboldt water produced bootleg whiskey which was trucked down to thirsty San Francisco. This was followed forty years later by a multibillion dollar marijuana industry, and Plonktown grocery stores sold books next to the cash register on how to grow better marijuana. The fog was a friend. It grew redwoods; hid things from people who shouldn't have been poking around anyway; and kept out some of the tourists.

The second fact of life in Plonktown was the scarcity of jobs. When Humboldt State University opened, Plonktown split into two rival groups for jobs, evenly divided. Currently there were 16,000 residents, including 8,000 students. This population split came to a crisis on the unlikely object of a small bird called the Northern Spotted Owl.

Local environmentalists had recently got a vast area of old growth redwood declared off limits to logging because it was the habitat of the owl, a bird on the federal endangered species list. This resulted in a significant loss of timber related jobs.

A timber workers' organization responded by contesting the permit for Humboldt County's largest entertainment event, the August music festival called Reggae on the River. The head of the timber workers pointed out that the location of the festival abutted an owl habitat and demanded an environmental impact report to determine whether reggae disturbed the birds.

"Maybe they prefer Sinatra?" sniffed the festival director. "This is the most ridiculous suit I ever heard of."

"Us rednecks are aware we're tacky and we're sorry to piss off the 7,000 yuppies come up to hear the music and sip their wine, but we're interested in protecting the spotted owl too, so it can be removed from the endangered species list and we can restore logging jobs."

"Oh come off it," the festival director snapped, "This is a pure attempt at lifestyle revenge. If you analyze the reggae festival demographics you'd find it's organized by and attracts many liberals who are against timber harvesting."

"Now maybe owls don't give a hoot about reggae. But we don't know that without an impact report."

"Oh, funny. This is the kind of thing those people think is funny, using the spotted owl against us, you can just see them poking each other in the ribs."

"We do have environmental laws and environmental laws are intended to be observed by everybody."

"I can't believe this act of pure vengeance, it won't help the timber industry stave off new regulations or win job retraining money; it will create resentment."

"Fair's fair."

It didn't help that a logger thrown out of work by the new Federal restrictions was not trained for the newly available jobs in systems analysis or environmental surveys. With the cutbacks in the lumber industry, HSU and its network of high tech industries became the major employers in Plonktown. So the locals considered the few service jobs that did exist—waiting tables, construction—theirs by right.

But with the cutback in college funding due to the state budget deficit, even these service jobs were now fiercely contested and usually taken by the students because they did better on tests. And some students liked the laid back Humboldt life style enough to take minimum wage jobs after they graduated, so that the bus driver might well have a Masters from HSU.

The locals viewed these young people, the men with single braids down their backs, the women fresh faced with their hair loose, as wealthy students supported by families in San Francisco and Los Angeles, playing at the Humboldt life. The students saw the locals as rednecks operating a good old boy network which froze them out of jobs because the locals guarded jobs for each other by passing the word on openings.

The locals tolerated the University. But Plonktown was not a tolerant town.

There was not much tolerance going on in Tom Harly's house. The house was located near the Old Plonktown Road leading to the lumber mills at Samoa and was a 900-square foot wood cottage built originally for mill workers, now painted dove gray and with an added glassed-in front porch, which Harly had lined with bookshelves. His books commingled democratically; some books upright, some books placed crosswise over the tops of the standing books, some books placed behind other books, so you had to know exactly where the book was to find it. At the rear of the house was a detached garage, housing Tom's black Toyota pickup and three of his son Yancey's bicycles. Next to the garage was a four foot high wooden structure with several platforms and some plastic water tubing, one of Yancey's abandoned projects.

The front door of the house was shut, but light shone through the fog from the glassed-in porch, and as Marge Fairweather rolled her mountain bike up the concrete walkway from the sidewalk she could see people in the living room through the small windowpanes: Tom Harly; Bart Poway from the gas station and his wife, Jenny; Mayor Elwood Stilton; Henry and Sally Richard; and Eric Linden, the bank manager.

Marge was a tall woman, muscular. She stood 5 feet 8 inches and weighed 130; the fabric of her Pendleton shirt strained across her square shoulders and fell loose in front of her jeans over a flat stomach. She pulled off a wool cap and ran her fingers through coarse red hair cut long at the nape and short on the sides and top. She took a deep breath. Some of the people inside that room weren't going to be happy with what she had to say, particularly Elwood and Bart.

She rolled her bike into the enclosed porch and tilted it carefully against the wall. She loved that bike. Tom said she was a menace on it, freewheeling down the hills and almost laying it down on the turns, yelling 'mudslap' as she slid across the puddles from the Plonktown rain.

"Because you know what this is," Mayor Elwood Stilton's voice boomed out of the house and he jabbed with a stubby finger, "This is Tom Harly's golden chance to say 'I told you so.'" Elwood stood next to Tom's bookcase, resting a ham sized elbow on a shelf.

Henry Richard said, "I don't understand how a big film company can have a contract and not do what they say. I mean, if I do that, I get sued. We're in that film they made. We gave them everything they asked for. It's been a week since my check bounced and I have a signed contract for $34,000 from them and now I don't ever expect to see my money."

"I have explained this at least three times," Eric Linden stared up at them through horn rimmed glasses, his lips pursed. He had a banker's face, pleasant, bland, hard to remember. "What's a contract if there's no money? All we've got is a bunch of framed black and white photos with the cast. They fixed it so the film company that made this film has no money. The bank's attorney did an asset search.

Some accountant down there called back and said even if we looked for twenty years we weren't going to find any assets. And even if we offered to let them film for nothing, the film crew will never be back here because they can always find a place that's cheaper to film."

"You mean these people can just do this and rip us off?" Sally Richard asked in a high piping voice.

That, Marge thought, was as good an opening line as she was likely to get. She checked her Timex wristwatch and entered, crossing the porch into a living room with two couches and a worn oriental rug. A pot belly stove was roaring in the corner and there was a kitchen to the right as big as the living room, and on the far wall was a hall leading to two bedrooms and a bathroom.

Most of the occupants wore jeans and lace-up gum bottom slush boots, together with heavy knit pullovers. Several of the women had donned beaded necklaces for the occasion, but only Sally Richard wore makeup.

Tom owned three matching dining chairs, painted white, which had been pressed into service. In addition, the two rigid white plastic chairs he used in the kitchen had been carried in, and the ergonomic stool he gave Yancey for use with his computer monitor, and the rolling secretary chair Yancey actually used. Marge placed a thick manila file of newspaper clippings taken from her bike basket on one of the dining chairs and started passing mimeographed sheets around.

"What the hell is this?" Bart Poway straddled one of Tom's wood kitchen chairs and his thick fingers fidgeted with the packet. "Pictures? I don't need magazine pictures of Herb Boland. Bastard was in my station every day for three weeks. I know what he looks like."

"Tom, if this is your idea of crowing, you and me is gonna dance." Stilton's voice boomed again. Clad in jeans and a soft leather jacket, Mayor Elwood Stilton looked like the lumberjack he had been in his youth. At 50 he was the largest and oldest person in the room, 6 feet 4 inches, and in the light from the wood stove, he looked as if he could still handle himself in a barroom brawl and would be delighted to demonstrate.

"Just because you didn't want the town to do the pilot, Harly, you think now you can crow." Bart said.

"Because Professor Tom Harly here," Elwood Stilton switched to his political declamatory voice, "he works up at Humboldt State University, he don't have to worry. Check comes regular; no matter he's against every damn thing."

"Come on, Elwood," Marge linked arms with Tom, "That's not fair. I'm a librarian at HSU and I get a regular check too and I thought making the TV pilot was a great idea."

"I asked Marge to do some research because I want us to do something about this film company." Tom Harly said.

Marge swiveled her eyes to Tom. Tom Harly was tall and thin and he had a collection of brightly colored suspenders including a pair with red paisley swirls which he wore today, because he didn't have enough of a butt to keep his pants up to his waist. He had pale skin and blue eyes and a pointy Vandyke beard and dark hair which he parted in the middle and he ran his fingers through it frequently. At Halloween he dressed as Dracula and all he needed was a cape and false plastic teeth.

"I've copied everything I could find, all the clippings. These are the people that ripped us off." Marge folded her arms akimbo. One hand was grimy from the bike and she noticed she'd made a thumbprint on the pristine tan of the file folder.

"I don't want to look at all this crap," Elwood said.

"Elwood, you pushed for us to go with these TV people," Henry said. "You brought them to my furniture store. If you think this isn't going to come up in the next election, well, I'm sorry."

"You want to split this town, Henry?" Elwood said. "You want to make this a political thing?"

"Henry, we all thought the TV show would bring the tourists to town." Sally Richard put her hand over Henry's, which stopped him from waving it. "The whole Chamber of Commerce voted for making the pilot, including you. It wasn't just Elwood."

"Damn right it wasn't."

21

"We should have made them pay up front." Tom Harly said.

"Tom, even Yancey enjoyed making the pilot, and there's nothing else I know can peel that kid off that computer screen of his," Marge said.

"Yancey is 15." Tom said. "His judgment's lousy. And it's hard to explain to a 15 year old the difference between bank robbery and what the film company did to us."

"Well, he loved being in that pilot and that counts for something," Marge said. "He's been pricing a laser printer, that's what he wanted to do with his money."

"He's not going to get any money," Tom said. "And he cancelled his regular trip this summer to see his mother on the East Coast so he could be in the pilot, and Sybil is having a fit."

"Jesus, Tom, even you can't blame Herb Boland for that." Marge noticed his mouth was closed in a stubborn line.

"What?" she asked.

"Nothing." He hesitated a second before answering.

"There's something else?"

"Nothing else," he said. "We were very naïve and just thought if we did what we were supposed to do, then they'd take care of their part."

"Tom."

"We're out of samosas." He scuttled to the kitchen.

Marge was watching him, which is the only reason she saw the tensing of his neck and back. Not for the first time, she wondered how he managed to stay so skinny in spite of his own gourmet cooking.

"Could we get back on the subject?" Jenny Poway was seated on the Oriental rug; her back slumped against the velvet front of the couch. "I wanted to put another bathroom in the house with our money, in case anybody's interested, before Bart found something to use it on in the damn gas station. So where does that get us?" At 28, Jenny Poway was much shorter than Marge or Sally. She stood 5 feet 2 inches and weighed 140. She favored her hair in a long brown pigtail, which smacked her rhythmically in the back when she nodded for emphasis, as she did now.

"Yeah, sure." Bart wadded up the copy of a magazine article which Marge had handed him and ringed it in the wastebasket.

"See, you just never listen to me." Jenny turned to the others for support. "I'll be talking to him and in the middle he'll interrupt with what he wants to say."

"Well, I can't get a word in otherwise, can I?"

"And after that he just stops listening, just like he did right now."

"Because you keep saying the same dumb thing."

"And then later when I ask him about so and so he doesn't even hear me."

"I'm trying to talk to you."

"Oh, now you're interested in talking to me, Mr. Big Business man. You never do what I tell you to. And everything I told you to do, it turns out we'd have made money."

"Jenny, for Christ's sake!"

"I told you to ask for money first from the film company. Didn't I tell you?"

"That's exactly the point," Henry Richard straightened up to full pouter pigeon posture. "I told Elwood and Bart the first time they brought this film offer before the Chamber, I said I am just not comfortable doing business with people from Southern California, get the money up front."

"Yeah, but Henry, you were at that meeting and all you could see was tourist bucks." Tom put down a blue ceramic plate of hot samosas. The savory smell of the samosas filled the small room. Bart edged across the room toward the plate.

"Well, we all know this would never have happened with people from around here." Elwood said. "These flakes from Southern California."

"Elwood, look up xenophobia. That's with an x, not a z." Marge said.

"That's the kind of fat lip remark you people from HSU make all the time." Elwood poked the air with an index finger the size of a sausage. "I happen to be a very good speller, 'cause they used to teach spelling back when I went to school, not like now."

"Good, then you'll be able to find out what it means."

23

"And that remark shows you don't know what we were trying to do for this town, Ms. Smartass."

"Okay, maybe I was out of line."

"You seen those guys on strike out at the paper mill on Samoa Island? They been out months, and it's raining on them and now they made a sort of shed to stand inside to get warm, with a fire in a barrel. And they're drinking some, to keep warm. And the outfit in New York bought the mill, they don't care. So we're down on taxes and it's costing the city to keep more cops on."

"Are we going to get stuck arguing again about the city having no money because of that strike?" Henry Richard rolled his eyes.

"We been stuck on that three months, since that strike begun." Elwood said. "Nothing's changed. We got people third generation timber workers and all of a sudden they can't feed their kids. City is short on money and we had to lay off the sanitation guys and contract out the garbage collection. If you don't think because we needed money was part of why we took on this film, well, you're just dumb."

"And I said be careful about the legal stuff." Henry said. "Now here we have the bank's attorney telling us if we had a payment schedule as we went along instead of waiting to the end, we'd have at least some of our money today."

"Yeah, everybody's great at pointing fingers and now the whole ruckus starts!" Elwood threw down his handful of newspaper clippings.

"Tom, you told us it was urgent and brought us here so we could admire magazine pictures of these bastards?" Bart said.

"Nope." Tom held up a hand, warding them off. "The first step is finding out about these guys, because we need to make them sorry they did this to us." Tom gestured at Elwood's file of clippings, now in a heap on the floor.

"The only thing to do is sue these people." Henry said.

"We can't sue them." Eric Linden said, "Because they fixed it so the film company has no money."

Marge took a deep breath. "Herb Boland and Broxton Films came here and made us promises and then they ran out. They shouldn't get away with that." She had spent two days of her carefully hoarded free time accumulating these files. Seemed like nobody was going to look at them, much less say thank you.

"Now, Marge, you weren't ripped off. This is just a cute excuse to crow. I don't see what business this is of a lady not involved." Elwood said.

"I live here and my town got ripped off." Marge said. "And I think we should get them back, not just roll over and be victims."

"Now we don't need that from some librarian--" Elwood said.

"But I'm into my second life, see. In this life I don't stand around and get ripped off, because being a victim is bad for you." Marge said. "So first I find out everything I can about them."

"What second life? I'm older than you are." Elwood walked over in front of Marge. She was tall, but he towered over her, forcing her to crane back her neck.

"Right again. At your stage of life I may be dead, so I may as well fight now." Marge did not step back. "We were guilty of small town ignorance; the first thing is to fix that. I summarized what I found out on those mimeographed sheets, including addresses and phone numbers for Boland and Diesel in Los Angeles, both unlisted, what a surprise."

"Just when did you get so big that you can tell us all what to do?" Jenny Poway glared at Marge.

"Does all this have something to do with getting money from that film company?" Sally's fluty voice.

"It sure does. We mount a classic guerilla action," Marge said, "which is the only thing to do when you have no power. When Boland and Diesel get unhappy enough, they'll pay us."

"Guerilla? This some kind of communist plan you got? 'Cause I already fought them suckers in Korea." Elwood said.

"Oh, now, that's great, guerilla? What are we, some kind of radicals?" Henry stood up. His legs were short and his steps were fussier than any other man in the room. "This is crazy. We do what people do, which is sue them."

"I have told you at least four times," Eric Linden raised his head, which had been in his hands, "that there is no money. Nothing to sue for. These people have been very clever. The bank's attorney took some time with this matter because we had so many checks up here that were bad."

"Yeah, and on top of everything, you bank guys are charging us now for the bounced checks the film company sent us!" Henry snapped.

"You know what, Marge; this sounds like more of that feminist bullshit I get lately with Jenny." Bart said.

"Bart, honey," Sally uncurled from the couch and stretched like a cat. Every man in the room flicked his eyes. "I don't hear you've got a better idea. Or you either, Mr. Mayor Elwood Stilton. So what I hear is, it's this idea or no idea."

All the yelling stopped.

"Gimme that stuff in that folder." Elwood said.

The top clipping was an article on Zoltan Diesel from **People** Magazine going back two years, titled "The Real Hollywood Clout." It showed pictures of Diesel in a tux being given an industry award; meeting with the cast of one of his TV series; driving his white Rolls; and a photo of him standing with his gardener in front of a specimen apple tree on his 2-1/2 acre Beverly Hills estate.

"You're not supposed to be able to grow apples in Southern California," Diesel was quoted. "It's not supposed to get cold enough. Actually, it's a matter of selecting the right location, the right microenvironment. Last year this tree gave over four bushels."

"And I've got articles on Herb Boland," Marge went through the papers in the folder, "about the series he directed for Nebula films with that Avery Ford, same actor was up here."

"I don't believe Herb is involved in this." Jenny Poway interrupted. "I think the film company lied to him too."

"That's about the third time you said that. You still taking Boland's side?" Bart Poway said.

"Herb tries to be responsible for everything, nobody on that crew helps him, they just sit around talking on their cell phones and some of them are really snotty, they think they're so big. The film company must have told him they had the money and then it turned out they didn't." Jenny stubbed out her cigarette. In seconds she lit another.

Tom wrinkled his nose and waved the smoke away from him. "That's bullshit, Jenny. Herb Boland made the agreements with us and then he walked out."

"Maybe he went to Los Angeles to find out, to ask about our money."

"If he's asking about our money, how come he didn't tell us what he's doing? That'll be the day, that one of them is up front with us." Bart twirled his hand.

"And, Elwood, I have no plan. What I'm asking for is plans." Tom finished.

"I don't see what it has to do with you either, Tom." Elwood said. "You didn't get ripped off."

"They ripped off my 15 year old kid. I don't like that."

"So what are we supposed to be," Jenny snapped. "Some kind of attack team? This is really silly."

"Let's not make everybody uncomfortable," Marge said. "The idea is to work together."

"Fine with me." Elwood said. "I grew up in a lumber camp and my daddy taught me never to take a licking without you get a piece of the guy back."

"Elwood, all this macho crap," Jenny's voice choked.

"Can I get a consensus? I don't get paid for this work on the City Council, you know." Eric Linden said. "And it took hours to get this agreement together. The legal agreement that releases the pilot's negative from civil court says that all creditors, including us, are to be paid from any net revenue the pilot might eventually earn."

"And it may never earn any revenue." Tom said.

"The bank's attorney and I were persuaded to accept that because it looked like the only hope for reimbursement."

"Which means we do nothing," Henry's mouth set in a thin line.

"I just said that, didn't I?" Sally said.

"Okay, so we've been scammed by a sophisticated producer," Tom said. "And so we weren't as suspicious as we should have been, because we didn't know about the film business, but we've learned."

"Yeah, what we've learned is, get all the money up front before you turn over your streets." Henry said.

"We have to deal with where we are now."

"And we should certainly have been warned about that by our Mayor. Too late now." Henry could not restrain a smirk at getting in the last word.

"You can argue all you want about suing Broxton Films, but it's not negotiable because the city's got no money for a lawsuit. That's all." Linden spread his hands, palms up.

"You guys mean to tell me we can't sue anybody?" Bart said. "Them guys in Eureka is gonna love this when they hear it."

"Oh, Jesus." Elwood rolled his eyes. "They already think we're all zonked on grass." Eureka, just south of Plonktown, was a blue collar town distinguished by the fact that State Highway 101 took an abrupt right hand dogleg in the middle of town. The town fathers had also chosen to change the local street name of the state highway from Broadway to 5th Street at the exact point of the dogleg. Therefore, unwary drivers who didn't make the abrupt right hand turn wound up at the grungy waterfront and also couldn't find 101 when they tried to come back. This turn was one of Elwood's favorite political targets. He called the turn the Eureka Mental Kink.

The muscular population of Eureka was suspicious of anything coming from Plonktown. Their view was it was their damn turn and it was going to stay the way it was. One Eureka City Council member called the mayor Ecogroovy City Elwood. But not to his face.

"Look, we can generate a lot of court costs which the town has no money for, but I've just explained there's nothing we can do legally, and I think we ought to forget it. There's no use flogging a dead horse." Linden said.

"Which is just what a limpdick like you would say." Elwood said.

"I am tired of trying to explain complex law to a retard."

"Okay, okay." Tom held up his hands. "Would you just listen for a minute?"

"I'll be happy to listen to you," Linden said, "which is a courtesy you have not extended to me."

"I don't see why we have to be so mean to each other." Jenny wiped her drippy nose with a tissue she took out of her sleeve.

"I don't need this; I have enough nonsense at the bank. What I may do is quit the City Council." Linden said.

"Linden, you can't quit, you been on the Council too long and nobody else knows what's happening with the finances, so shut up." Elwood said.

"Marge made a complete set of this file for everybody." Tom handed out the stapled copies. "Dammit, we weren't born yesterday. They're going to be surprised if we go after them and annoy them enough to make them deal with us. But this is going to take thought. Nobody's expected to come up with an idea tonight."

"I have made my suggestion. Anything else is insanity. That's all." Eric Linden stood up, snapping the belt on his raincoat with a flourish. He wore taps to protect the bottoms of his shoes, and his footsteps were a cannonade as he stalked across the floor and headed out into the rain, glaring at Elwood as he passed him.

"So what do you suggest we do?" Bart Poway said. "Maybe you'd like us to go lean on them? Break their legs?"

"Oh, funny, that's really hilarious. Bart, you're being a pain in the ass tonight." Tom said.

Bart Poway jumped to his feet, a declamatory voice, "Folks, you've seen Rambo, we've got Tombo."

"Jesus," Tom looked at the wall, "maybe Poway is right. Maybe this idea is really crazy. I was going to point out that Bart was an enthusiastic supporter of the pilot from the beginning, but I don't feel like getting into anything more with him tonight."

"Look, we're all tired. Could we cool it for tonight, and meet in a week, and everybody brings his own plan to sting Diesel and Boland?" Tom said.

"Well, why didn't you say we were going to do that before?" said Bart. "We're all sitting here."

"You didn't ask before." Tom said.

"Another goddam educated idiot."

Tom strode abruptly into the kitchen.

"What?" Marge followed him.

Tom was standing up because all the kitchen chairs were in the living room. "Because if I stayed in the room with Bart I was going to say something I'd be sorry for. These guys are never going to get it together."

It took less than an hour to prove him wrong.

Chapter Four

"If you really want to know what I think," Tom Harly stretched for the spices above his large, enameled tan 1927 gas stove, "There was a mix-up at the hospital when you were born."

"Tom, for God's sake, what a thing to say to the kid." Marge was setting the table, wearing an outrageous red silk robe embroidered with a yellow dragon, over a long sleeved tee shirt and dungarees, and shuffle stepping to a tape of Aerosmith.

"And Sybil didn't realize because she was drugged."

"Tom!"

"And then they had this leftover kid they wanted to get rid of."

"Tom, that's enough, I don't think that's funny."

"And they gave me the wrong kid."

"Mellow out, Marge." Yancey Harly cueballed across the kitchen linoleum to the table on his secretary chair. "He's been claiming that for years." He glanced at the pot on the stove.

"I could not have a kid who survives on microwaved burritos. My genes would murder the burrito genes." Tom said.

The rain was coming in earnest now, Plonktown rain, coming sidewise, banging on the kitchen window, which was steamed with the cooking, the wind making it rattle in its frame. On the narrow painted windowsill Tom grew basil, cilantro, and mint, in six inch square pots.

"What's this?" Yancey switched to peeling an orange. At 15, Yancey wore his brown hair shaped like a bowl over his pudgy face, clunky square glasses low on his nose. He stood 5 feet 5 inches and weighed 156 lbs. and he was wearing a tee shirt with a drawing of a rigid penis and the legend, 'Safe sex. Wrap that Rascal.'

"Probably a disaster." Tom Harly peered in the pot. "The recipe said the sauce should get thick."

"Dad, do you seriously expect me to eat that chicken in brown gook?"

31

"Brown gook? Gook? This is coq au vin, you little turd, my coq au vin is the toast of the North Coast."

"What are the little brown things floating over there?" Yancey pointed in the pot.

"Dried mushrooms which I have reconstituted by putting them in water."

"Oh."

"Just listen to the way you say that. When you get to college and have to survive on dorm food," Tom judiciously tasted the tip of his wooden spoon, "you'll come back here begging for these delicacies, which you've thumbed your nose at for the last three years."

"I'll stick to the burrito."

"That is, of course, if you make it into M.I.T. without calculus."

"I have calculus."

"You didn't take it."

"I don't have to take it. They give you a test. If you pass the test, they give you credit for calculus, and I aced that test."

Tom Harly looked at his son. The kid probably had aced the damn test. He seemed to be some kind of math genius, but Tom figured he'd better go to Yancey's school and check anyway.

Where the hell had that talent come from? He was fair at math, but nothing like Yancey, who seemed to inhale the stuff. And Sybil, Yancey's mother, could barely balance a check book. As close as Tom could figure, Yancey memorized algebra formulas the way other people memorized multiplication tables, so when he started working a math problem, he started on a whole higher level.

"Did you call your mother? She still wants to have some time with you. She said maybe Thanksgiving."

"Dad, I don't feature what you're all upset about. I don't see much of mom when I go east anyway. She has to work a lot of nights now she's department head."

"Yancey, your mother's life is different from ours, but she's still upset about you not coming east this summer."

Yancey took a handful of pretzels, his chewing crunching across the kitchen as he removed a microwaved burrito. The smell of the burrito mingled with the garlicky smell of the coq au vin and the smell of the wood stove in the living room.

"Mom and I go out to dinner a lot. I get to order what I want, big steaks and everything. That part's fun. The rest of it's boring."

"So you figure what to do with yourself while your mother's working; come on, Yance."

"You know that mug I made in ceramics for mom for last Christmas? It was for her to drink her coffee at work. Anyway, she gave it back last time I was there. Said she already had enough mugs."

"So where's the mug?"

"I dumped it at Kennedy airport. I mean, it wasn't for me."

"Oh, Jesus, I'm sorry, Yance."

"The bad thing is, the only fast terminal I can use is at her office and the lady runs the computers there keeps watching over my shoulder. I hate it when they do that. I think she thinks I'm going to break something."

"Yancey, you have to visit your mother, so let's not start."

"Dad, last time the computer lady asked if I had clean hands. I thought she was going to ask me to show her."

"Yancey, I can't handle this right now." Tom slammed the wooden spoon on the counter with a splat. "Okay?"

"Okay, okay. Hey," Yancey thumbed through Marge's file, "here's a picture of Herb Boland. You know, the guy who directed the TV pilot. What is this stuff?"

"Yancey, just drop it," Tom roared, "go play with your computer."

"I do not," Yancey said with dignity, "play with a computer. And I asked a polite question. I think I deserve a polite answer."

"Stop dripping orange juice on the damn file!"

"Dad, what's with you?" Yancey stared at Tom; his face and neck turned red as he dropped the file on the table. His

33

glasses misted over. Suddenly his Joe Cool teenager mask cracked and Marge glimpsed the child behind the teen.

With a visible effort, Tom stopped. "Okay, okay, I don't want to snap at you. I got the bright idea we should figure how to sting those film guys because they ripped us off so bad, and Marge researched them so we could know what we're dealing with. She found out a lot about them."

"Marge is a real pisser when she gets mad."

"Yancey, could you manage a little respect?"

"I have got respect. That was a compliment. I think it's a great idea. Mellow out, Dad, I still don't understand why you're so pissed."

Tom Harly picked up a heavy black cast iron pot, burned his fingers, and sloshed coq au vin on the stove, swearing. He had a collection of black cast iron pots and maintained it meticulously, seasoning it regularly. One of his first arguments with Sybil was when she scoured one of his pots and he had to re-season it. "Because the scam idea was mine, and I told everybody to think about doing something."

"Okay. So?"

"First of all, everybody hated the idea, and besides, now I've been thinking all day and I can't come up with a damn thing I could do. Makes me feel dumb and I don't deal well with feeling dumb." Tom broke a leaf off the aloe plant he kept in a pot on the back splash of the stove and rubbed some on his finger.

"Yance," Tom stopped. "Yance, look, your mother is a really good businesswoman. I mean, we've had our differences, and the divorce and all, but I've got to give her that. And you did this film and you didn't go see her and now their check bounced. I just think if this had been while you were with her, she'd have had the money for you up front."

"Dad," Yancey spoke slowly in a speaking to obtuse parent voice, "If I'd been with her I'd have been in New York and I wouldn't have been in the film at all. Do we have more Cokes in the garage?"

"Yeah," Tom said, "but it's pouring."

"I'll run fast, Dad," Yancey said, running through the kitchen door. The "Dad" had a good effect and Tom quieted down.

"What's really bothering you?" Marge had been listening at the kitchen doorway and she stepped back into the kitchen after Yancey ran through.

Tom remained stubbornly silent.

"Okay, you can tell me to shut up, but I've never heard you talk to Yancey that way. You always treat him almost like another adult, more like brothers than father and son."

Tom walked back to the stove, his back curiously stiff. "So that means you think my parenting style sucks, right?"

"Hey, that's not what I said."

"Because I think my parenting style works. Yancey is not a bad kid."

"I didn't say he was. Tom, what's wrong with you?"

"Because Sybil is on to me, that I'm a lousy parent."

"Tell me what's going on. I have to know. We're either up front with each other or we're not."

"Yeah. Okay, Yancey told Sybil his check bounced and Sybil called me and said it was a good thing I was a teacher because I'd lose my ass in business. She said it was the wimp factor."

"Hello? You were the one told the City Council not to do the film, remember?" She walked to him, picked up his hand and examined the burn.

"She said I'm running true to form because I send out some kind of psychological signal that encourages people to shit on me."

"Oh come on, does the whole town send out a signal?" Marge dropped his hand. "Because the whole town got screwed."

"Anyway, I found out Sybil sent Yancey to some big time psychologist last time he was with her; he didn't tell me. Guy said it might affect him to be with me. I might make him a model of low expectations."

"Oh, Jesus." Marge slumped in one of the white kitchen chairs.

"So now, here he has his first job and he tells her the check bounced. She says I'm teaching him to be a shit magnet, like me, that there are people who are shit magnets. And she wants him to come live with her. Until he goes to M.I.T. After that he'll be on the East Coast anyway."

"Tom," Marge tilted the chair on two legs, "Yancey won't go. It's all you can do to get him to Sybil's for two weeks. You can't deliver him like a Christmas turkey."

"Deliver who?" Yancey came back with a Coke.

Damn, thought Marge, for a kid who was always in his own world, he sure could zero in on the one thing you didn't want him to hear.

"It has to do with making money, which is important to your mother." Tom stamped across the kitchen back to the stove.

"That part I can understand; I think it's a female thing." Marge nodded. "When I went back to school I wanted a course in poetry. I was good at it, which was a surprise, and I got a couple of poems published."

"I didn't know that." Tom came back to sit down next to her. "How come you never told me? Can I see some of your stuff?"

"I gave it up because it was when my mother was sick and I needed to do something that makes money, and poetry doesn't."

"You could write now."

"I don't want to do something for no money. That's why I say it's a female thing. 'Money dignifies what is frivolous if unpaid for.' "

"Virginia Woolf, right?"

"It's great being with someone teaches Lit Crit. Look, in our society money means respect and no money means no respect."

"I agree about the money, and that's why I want to bug the film guys until they pay." Tom said.

"Well, I don't know about Diesel," Yancey hooked his feet around the legs of the secretary chair and started eating the burrito, "but this article says Boland gets residuals from

Nebula Films. How about if we put a virus in the operating system that pays his residuals?"

"A what?"

"Dad, a virus." The teen was back; 15-year-old boys have a short recovery time, and Yancey performed a teenage rollup of eyes. "You've got to be the only person in California doesn't know about computer viruses. I mean, do you put your head out the door?"

"Wait, I know what viruses are." Marge extended a stiff index finger. "They're instructions deliberately planted when the computer is communicating over telephone lines. They're not put there by the person operating the computer. Somebody else can change what your computer does."

"Sure," Yancey sprayed out burrito bits. Tom closed his eyes and shook his head. "If I can get into an electronic mail computer used by execs at Nebula Films and figure out how to bypass their operating system security, then I can modify the accounting software and then every time they send a statement to Boland the error will happen."

"But they've got to catch that." Tom dished the coq au vin into two ironstone soup bowls.

"Naw, they might catch it once, Dad, but they're not going to catch it most of the time. What if we instruct it to add another zero every time it prints Boland a statement?"

"Jesus Christ," Tom put down the spoon, "can you do that? I mean, don't they have safeguards?"

"Well, you can't make him really get paid more," Yancey said. "They'd catch that right away. But a mistake in the statement? That could go on forever."

"This is fantastic," Marge was slurping coq au vin. "Yancey, you're crazy to miss this. It's impossible to be upset after a meal like this," she added pointedly.

"So then Boland would think he has more money than he has. But couldn't they catch you? I mean, it sure as hell must be illegal."

"No way." Yancey ignored Marge. "The thing about a virus is, once one is in their system it's just left there and it's hard to tell it's there, much less who put it there."

"Yancey, it can't be that easy."

37

"I didn't say it would be easy. They'll have layers of security. It'll take me a while to figure, but I've got this neat new program to find predictable passwords. I wonder if I could do it? It'd really be fun," he said, all sweetness and light now that he'd gotten his way.

The doorbell rang.

"Sorry I acted so pissed tonight," Bart Poway's voice was slurred coming from the dark porch, as if he had been drinking, "so I'm gonna explain."

"Yeah, Bart, what the hell was going on with you? I've never seen you like that." Tom stepped back and put on the porch light.

"Would you shut up, because if I don't tell you now I don't know if I'm gonna be able to tell you."

"Bart, if you don't want to tell me, hell, don't. I was pissed off tonight too."

"Jenny told me she's pregnant and she thinks Herb Boland is the father."

"Bart!" Tom stopped. "She actually told you that?"

"She's been reading a lot of books lately about honesty in a marriage."

"Uh, really, or is this just you been drinking?"

"What the hell, I asked her did he offer her a part or something in the damn pilot. And she started to bawl and said it was his intensity."

"His what?"

"That he seems to live different than we do, as if we're all half dead. Honest to God, it's too early for the change, but I swear she's going whacko."

"Uh, Bart, maybe you shouldn't be telling me this, this is personal--"

"And that she wanted to feel alive, the way he is, just for a little while."

"I don't know what to say to you."

"Look, I'm not as smart as you guys." Bart said. "But that Rolls Diesel was driving? In the picture in the article Marge gave me? Well, I worked a couple years at a fancy dealership, so I know something about those cars. I got an idea, but it's gonna take more than one person, so I'm gonna need a couple men to pull it off."

"Whatever you need. Just tell us what we have to do. And I'm in the middle of figuring out something with Yancey right now. Wait a minute, that's the phone." It took Tom two more rings to answer, because he had to run from the front door.

"Tom," Elwood Stilton boomed on the phone, "I got a real good idea. I'll show Eric Linden who's a retard. But I'm going to need a couple men."

"So we can pull it off." Tom said. Jesus, he thought, talk about déjà vu.

"Huh? Oh, right." Stilton said.

"We'll have to ask the others," Tom said, "because the original idea was each person comes up with his own scam."

"Well, it ain't going to work that way. We're all going to have to help each other, teamwork."

"Just a minute." Tom put the phone on the table and ran to the door. "Bart, Elwood's on the phone. Wait a minute." He ran back to the phone.

"So we're all going to work together and we're going to have to decide on timing." Stilton lowered his voice. "Whose scam goes first. Because we'll lose the element of surprise after the first operation. The enemy will be alerted."

"The enemy?" Tom said. "Operation?" He switched the phone to his other ear.

"Are you going to let me tell you this or not?" Bart called from the door.

"It's going to be exactly like planning a military campaign." Stilton said, his voice taking on a military timbre. "Now I happen to have done a lot of reading about that. Sort of a hobby of mine, reading military books."

"Military books?"

"You know, I was with the Marines during the Korean. Got out in '53. The forgotten war. You hear all about these Vietnam guys, but when was the last time you heard about a Korean vet getting depressed or shooting up a lobby?"

"Elwood, about the scam, I don't know how much time we have available."

"In the Marines there's one idea they drum into you. It's that time spent on reconnaissance is never wasted. So what time we got is what time it takes."

"You're not listening to me; nobody listens to me. Jenny is talking about nobody listens to her, what about me?" Bart said. "Just do me a favor, okay? Don't repeat what I told you." He slammed the front door.

"What the hell?" Marge came out from the kitchen.

"Uh, Elwood, I thought we'd do something relatively simple."

"Wait'll you hear this idea." Stilton rolled on. "It's so beautiful you're going to cry. Got the idea from one of those articles Marge copied. So you wasn't never in the army?"

"I was in graduate school."

"A lot of them got around it that way." Elwood's voice was dark.

"Elwood, for Christ's sake."

"Well, lemme tell you, son, this is gonna be the most fun you ever had in your entire life."

Chapter Five

The Friday morning hush in the Beverly Hills streets north of Sunset Boulevard was broken only by the thwack of tennis balls and the sighing of silver olive trees whose branches moved in the breeze against the deeper green of the tall pines. Most of the estates were walled, so that you couldn't see into them from the winding city streets, except right at the electronically operated gates. The setbacks between the walls and the city curbs were covered by foot-high ivy thick enough to discourage the footfall of the impecunious. Occasionally an electronic gate would slide open and a car would glide onto the street. The last one Tom Harly had seen was an Excalibur.

It was the fifth of November and Tom Harly was clinging to a telephone pole at the mouth of a service alley, wearing a coverall with the name of a cable TV service stitched into it.

"Why me?" Tom said into his walkie talkie, his other hand white with the effort of holding the pole tight. "I mean, why the hell am I up here on a telephone pole? I nearly broke my shinbone."

"Shut up." Stilton's voice came on the walkie talkie. "You're up there because you the only one of us has absolutely no experience lumbering."

"Elwood, it's not something I thought I would need."

"That's what you said when I explained my plan about Diesel's trees."

"And I still think so."

"All the time I been mayor, you had a lot to say about cutting trees, Tom. Every damn council meeting you had something to say. You think anybody can cut down a tree. Sure, start hacking a wedge out of one side and the tree will come down, you bet. But try laying an eighty foot pine out along a narrow clearing, staying away from power lines and not killing yourself."

"I don't need to know how."

"Seems awful simple, but I did it for twenty years and I'm just beginning to understand what it's all about. So let me tell you, you don't know how to cut a tree."

"I didn't say I knew how to cut a tree. You were the one said you needed help."

"Probably grew up in a movie house or something. Get off the walkie talkie and just check your belt is hooked on like I showed you."

"But I get dizzy when I look down." The pole vibrated to a hum in the heavy wires and Tom stiffened.

"You ain't supposed to be looking down! You're supposed to be watching inside of Diesel's place."

"But I can't even see much."

"There's only one thing you're supposed to see."

"Hold it." Tom said. "The electric gate is opening. I think he's driving out now."

"Shut up, don't let him see you talking. Right on time." Stilton said.

"I see the car."

"We figured it'd take Diesel two hours to drive to that golf tournament in Ojai."

"It's him all right," Tom tried to cover his mouth with his hand and almost fell off the pole, "driving the Rolls."

"See, that's just what I meant about reconnaissance. You did good, finding out he'd be at that golf tournament."

"It was Marge. The tournament's for the Venice Free Clinic and one of the magazine articles said he was on their board. So she called the golf club, said she was a reporter and needed to know who would be playing, and there he was."

"Okay" Stilton said. "8:45 A.M. We'll give him twenty minutes to make sure he's clear and don't come back for anything."

At 9:05 A.M. a large green pickup truck pulled up to the electronic gate Tom Harly had been watching. Three men in overalls and hard hats got out. The crew boss rang the bell, which was answered by a Mexican houseboy.

"What you want?"

The crew boss flapped a work order at him and strode through the gate.

"Wait a minute, Mr. Diesel, he don't tell me."

"Well you can read the work order, can't you?" the crew boss said.

"Mr. Diesel, he tell me when there's workers coming and he didn't."

"Because we didn't know we could get here today, but we got a cancellation," the crew boss said. "Up to you, but Diesel's so hot to trot he already paid us, and if I have to pull my men off now I don't know when I can reschedule; could be weeks from now, we're booked solid."

The houseboy paused. "Well," he said, "if he paid you."

"Right." The crew boss waved the truck through the gate. The men unpacked equipment. Each started a chain saw. The houseboy tried to say something else. Then he put his hands over his ears and ran back to the kitchen. Each workman selected a tree and started cutting.

Henry Richard grabbed the handle of his saw and chose a place on the trunk beneath intersecting branches, the way Elwood had showed him. He hoped he could hold the saw horizontal, because it was practically bucking out of his hands. The shriek of the saw was so loud it was painful. The cut wood Elwood made them practice on in Plonktown was a lot easier, because it was already parallel to the ground.

Elwood said he'd come over and check them after they got going. Where was he? Henry risked a look sidewise over at Elwood and the saw started up wood and jammed, nearly knocking Henry off his feet. A gear or something was slipping.

"What the hell are you doing, Henry?" Elwood ran to his side and flipped the switch on the handle of Henry's saw. "Jesus, now we're going to have to pull it out."

"I was trying to see when you were coming."

"Put your hands on the handle and pull, godammit. It's going to take two of us to get the damn thing out."

"I'm pulling."

"Bart, get over here," Elwood roared. The three of them pulled.

"Uhhn," Henry grunted, and then another "Uhhn" as, with a tearing sound, the blade of the saw came out of the tree.

"Henry, just watch what you're doing, wouldja?" Elwood strode back to his tree. "I mean, this is nothing. These are healthy trees. You try it when a tree's got beetles. Then you never know how that sucker's gonna fall."

"Beetles? This tree could have beetles?"

"When I was lumbering I was taking down a hundred trees a year, and every once in a while something happens that's unexpected, but Henry, you're more unexpected than I got room for today."

Henry's groin hurt from pulling the saw. Could you get a hernia from pulling something horizontal, like you could from lifting something heavy? He hoped the damn tree would fall away from him, the way Elwood said it would, and not crush him like a bug, which was one of the things he'd been going to ask Elwood before, but now didn't dare.

Elwood came back and stood behind him. "Slice a pie wedge. That's the undercut, out of the side of the tree. Then use a wedge on the other side to tip the tree."

"A pie wedge," Henry croaked.

"Remember, the undercut is like the sights on a rifle. Tells you where the tree is gonna fall. Keep your pie wedge clean. You get those pie wedges crossing, the trunk can split right up to the top and half of it can land on you."

Henry flipped the toggle switch. The motor began again with a steady high-pitched whine, which was a lot better than the shriek it had been making before.

Henry, who could see his saw progress across the diameter of the tree, began to feel better. He spread his legs and dug into the earth with the heels of the ankle-high full grain leather boots he'd bought, standing the way Elwood and Bart were standing. Next to him Bart was holding steady with his saw and was almost clear across his tree. The smell of cut tree mingled with the loamy smell of the trees and the gasoline smell from the saw.

Abruptly there was a sharp crack. For a terrified second Henry thought Diesel might be back and shooting at them.

This time he remembered to flip off the toggle switch before he turned.

The crack was the snap of Elwood's tree trunk, which fell with a ferocious thump, shaking the earth and raising a cloud of dust. Elwood straddled it like a horse and started cutting it into three foot sections. He seemed to alternately get off the tree and check the cut he was making, sometimes giving it a sharp blow to sever a piece. Next to him a pile of cut logs was growing.

Henry grinned, turned his saw back on, and began to softly sing 'John Henry' which he had learned because of the name from an old Electra folk music record of Sally's. There was something to be said for working with your hands in the open, the camaraderie of good men. He liked the feel of the checkerboard wool shirt he was wearing, and the faded jeans, even the green tin helmet Elwood got for him. There was more to this tree business than he had suspected. There really was a method of cutting.

Three hours later Elwood's walkie talkie crackled to life. A red MG started up the curving street to the electric gate.

"Watch out! It's that actor, Avery Ford, that was in the pilot." Tom Harly said on the walkie talkie.

"Jesus, he'll recognize us!" Bart Poway said.

"No, he won't." Stilton said.

"Hell he won't, I was in the scene with him." Henry said in a stage whisper. He shut off his chain saw and ran to Stilton. He could picture Ford alerting the houseboy, the houseboy calling the police, him having to call Sally.

"He wasn't looking at you, Henry, was he?" Stilton said. "He was looking at the twat he was supposed to be in love with when they was filming him."

"My God, the whole thing's going wrong." Henry's arms were windmilling. "We're all going to be arrested."

"Stop jumping around. Whatever you do, don't stop working. And keep your head down."

Henry put a hand on Stilton's chest. "Sally said I should come with you guys because she's still mad about that second trust deed on the store, but I knew this wasn't going to work."

"Hold on to your nerve because if you blow it for us all I'm going to kill you myself and you won't have to worry about Ford." Stilton knocked Henry's hand off. "Henry, I promise you he won't recognize you. To him you were a fly on the wall."

"Please, you guys, listen, you never listen to me."

"For Christ's sake, Henry!"

"Henry, get back to the damn tree!" Bart said. "Now! And turn on your saw."

"What can they do to you if you cut down a tree?" Henry said. "I mean, it can't be all that serious, right?"

"And will you for Christ's sake watch what you're doing with that chain saw?" Bart said. "You move your hands when you talk, and you're gonna cut off your leg or something more important."

"Henry, we look different in these outfits." Stilton said. "Just keep your head down and keep working."

Henry retreated to his tree. For a moment he stood tense and motionless. Then he swung around and turned on his saw.

The man who drove through the gate was in his 40's, almost gaunt in his good looks. His face was long and narrow, with high cheekbones, an almost oriental cast. Avery Ford looked like a Hollywood stereotype of a TV star; the pompadour of hair thinning, but carefully combed and hair-sprayed to look windblown, the acute profile still holding, and under the eyelashes the scars of an eye job done by the most expensive cosmetic surgeon in Beverly Hills. His hands on the wheel were large, projecting from a jacket made of buttery soft buckskin leather with thongs up the sleeve.

Ford smiled and swung a leg over the side door of the MG, then stopped and gaped at the workmen. The pungent smell of new cut lumber was all around, but Ford smelled of peppermint.

The estate looked like a scare picture from the Sierra Club. All the trees surrounding Diesel's house were gone, the rolling hills bristling with stumps where the trees had been crosscut. The stripped down ultramodern white house, which had been discreetly screened by the trees, now stood on its knoll, naked to view in all directions, resembling an enormous fast food clamshell box.

"What in hell's going on?" Ford asked the houseboy. He gestured toward the workmen.

The houseboy shrugged. "I dunno. Mr. Diesel, he tell them."

"Look, I told Diesel I'd be coming up today to talk about a plan for marketing the pilot for the Plonktown series. Diesel said to come on up."

"He up at the golf." The houseboy said.

"Diesel told them to cut down the trees? Look, man, he's a freak about those trees. Are you sure? Because something's wrong."

"You gotta talk louder, I can't hear nothing, all that noise."

"When is Diesel coming back?" Ford shouted.

"He up at the golf all day." The houseboy turned back to the house.

"Bastard." Ford walked toward Henry, who was intently sawing, his head down.

"We got a problem." Stilton said into his walkie talkie.

Back at the telephone pole, Stilton's voice came through the receiver.

"What?" yelled Tom Harly. "What problem?"

"Mister?" a small voice rose from the ground at the foot of Tom's telephone pole.

Tom looked down. A boy of eight was looking up at him.

"Mister, you're not doing anything."

"What?"

"You're not doing anything. I've been watching since I came home from school. You're just sitting there."

"Uh, it's my lunch hour." Tom said.

"But it's not lunch time."

"I have lunch when I can."

"What?" Stilton said on the walkie talkie.

"Not you." Tom said and shut off the walkie talkie.

"Because our cable went out last night while I was watching a movie," the boy said, "and it was the best part."

"Oh." Tom said.

"The bad guy had the girl and he said he was going to cut off her fingers."

"Sounds exciting."

"And then the cable went out. So are you fixing it?"

"Jason." A young dark haired maid came to the wall. "Come in."

"In a minute."

"Your sandwich and milk are ready," the maid said, "and you know you mama don't want you disturbing the workmen when they busy."

"Okay, okay." Jason turned back to Tom Harly. "Tonight's 'Wrath of Khan' and tomorrow's no school, so my mom said I could stay up."

"Your sandwich is getting cold." Tom said.

"It's salami."

"Jason, that means now." The maid said.

"Okay." The boy ran to a gate in the wall, then turned back. "I sure hope you get it fixed."

Tom switched back the walkie talkie as soon as the gate closed. The first voice he heard was Elwood's. Tom could hear him over the noise of the saws. He was saying, "We can't be responsible for that car, you leave it there."

Henry hunched over the branches he was cutting.

"You can see there's branches falling all around," Stilton said. "If we scratch that car our insurance don't cover it. Specially a classic, like that MG."

"This is a typical Diesel performance," Ford tossed his head and patted his hair, "total disregard of anybody else's time, I mean, I called him and he said to come up. Whatever's going on, he can solve it."

Henry's heart settled back in his chest as he listened to the receding snarl of the MG.

"Jesus," Bart said, "why'd you take a chance talking to him?"

"Because if he stayed here, sooner or later he'd recognize one of us," Elwood said. "And we wouldn't be able to get out. The Beverly Hills cops are fast."

Henry suddenly realized that in threatening Ford's MG Elwood had done the one precisely right thing. Maybe Elwood really could have commanded a Marine contingent; he certainly had the balls for it.

The sweat on Henry's face felt icy, and he noticed the wrist that was holding the saw was beginning to burn. Henry wouldn't have believed a wrist could burn, but his was. He took a short step toward the next tree. The backs of his legs were beginning to bother him too, and he hadn't even finished his branches pile. Beside him, eyes on their saws, the others had growing piles of logs next to them.

Henry bit his lips and leaned into his saw. Maybe it would kill him, but he was not going to be left behind.

By dusk they were all moving like wooden puppets. None of them was used to this kind of killing physical labor. Even Bart must have taken a break at the station from time to time to talk to customers. Now Bart's face was gray with fatigue and Elwood limped on an old leg injury.

Henry was beyond pain, his eyes glazed.

An alarm went off on Elwood's wrist watch. He shut it almost immediately, so he must have been waiting for it. He took off his hard hat to wipe his brow, looked around the Diesel estate, and smiled. Henry looked around too.

In the raking Edward Hopper light of sunset, the estate was barren. They had clear-cut every tree, so that the area looked like a stubbled forest ready for sowing. Periodically the lush grass was interrupted by what looked like flat saucers of various diameters, the tree stumps. And where the trunks had been dragged into a pile, the grass was worn, like a well used area on a carpet.

"Second step," Elwood bellowed and started for the truck. Henry and Bart followed him, straddle legged with weariness, looking like a scene from "Night of the Living Dead." Elwood rolled a backhoe down a ramp from the truck and, for the next half hour, trenched the property in a large crisscross pattern, the other two following and sowing small green culms at careful intervals about a foot down into the soil. Occasionally one or the other of them swore at the pain in his back, and they were more than happy to collapse in the truck while Elwood retraced his steps, filling the trenches with dirt.

The shadow of the wrought iron gate was almost twelve feet long when the crew carefully loaded the trunks and the large branches onto the pickup truck and stacked the small branches and leaves in a pile near the trash.

"You guys sure made a lot of noise." The houseboy said when he opened the gate. "I got a headache. But at least you clean up after. If the workmen don't clean up, Diesel, he makes me do it."

"Sure thing." Elwood waved as the truck pulled out and made a turn at the end of the street to circle the block. None of the men looked back at a white object placed near the crosscut trunk of one of the trees.

At the end of the service alley they stopped to pick up Tom Harly, who could barely bend his knees after a day spent hanging on the telephone pole.

"My God, I was scared." Tom collapsed in the truck. "The private security patrols kept passing and I thought any minute we'd get arrested."

"For attacking a tree?"

"Elwood, we did it!" Tom said. "We actually did it."

"You got the easy part, Tom," Bart complained. "Just hanging up on a pole all day while we had to saw."

"Elwood, it's a good thing you made us practice." Henry said. "We'd never of been able to cut all those trees in one day."

Bart leaned back on the seat. "Everything I own hurts, but you know what? I'm awake now, and some coffee would taste real fine. In fact, I'm starving."

"Me too." Tom Harly said. "I'm not scared now. I could eat a steak. I could eat a cow. You know, I can't believe it. It doesn't seem possible we really did it."

"Told you you'd be glad you come." Elwood said. "Nothing like a well scouted operation; cut down the surprises."

They drove on, then, looking like just a truck full of dusty workmen after a day laboring on the estates in Beverly Hills. A close observer, however, might have noted their expressions of serene satisfaction.

"What now?" Tom asked.

"First some food." Elwood removed his hard hat for the day and placed it on the floor of the truck cab. "Tomorrow we sell this load to the Exotic Wood Emporium down in Fortuna. Should bring us top dollar, rare woods like this, gorgeous stuff. And I'm the guy knows exactly how much it should bring." He wiped the sweat off his brow with his sleeve and put on a Humboldt Crabs baseball cap. Then he grinned and dug a burly elbow into Bart Poway.

"Hey," he said. "Down payment."

Chapter Six

Avery Ford had several peculiarities.

He was curious by nature and as he guided the MG down through the hills away from Diesel's estate the puzzle of the trees kept bothering him, but he tried to put it out of his mind. Like most things he tried to put out of his mind, the puzzle came back insistently. Mind control. He needed to get better at mind control.

But cutting trees wasn't in character for Diesel, and Ford was an actor who was bothered by actions out of character.

Ford had acted in four movies with British stars. Like most good actors, he was a quick study, and he had come out of those movies with two skills he had learned from the Brits: a slight clip to his diction, so his speech patterns had an international flair; and the ability to present a calm façade when he was furious. This discipline enabled him to ignore chaos on the sets, screaming arguments among the co-stars and even personal slights, and to single-mindedly pursue his goal, which currently was the vigorous marketing of the series he'd just made in Plonktown.

All with a smile, a gleaming, even-toothed smile, which he knew was one of his best features.

The exterior calm when he was furious did not, however, come without a price. The strain of containing his emotions and never losing his upper class cool had brought Ford a series of depressions, which he fought off and which occasionally required professional help. And it had lost him three wives.

Ford had an ability to adjust, chameleon like, to his surroundings. This was especially true of his wives, and as he lived with each wife his habits, interests, and even his car, changed. When a marriage broke up, he sold all of his personal belongings, down to his sports equipment and clothes, and remained in a state of suspension until his next love interest.

He met his first wife at the Palomino, a country and western music bar in the San Fernando Valley, one year when he had a minor role in a country music film. Her family owned horse property in the Valley, and she was tanned, sandy-haired, and interested in drapes. They rented a house with a pool near Rinaldi Street.

She worked as an accountant and they had two children and he spent Saturday afternoons flying model planes with his son at Sepulveda Reservoir. Saturday mornings were spent shopping at various supermarkets, newspaper coupons in hand, and he remarked to a friend at this time that fresh fruit was ridiculously expensive because the kids didn't eat it and it went rotten before you knew it.

He drove a brown Oldsmobile station wagon and wore light colored polyester suits with vests and a heavy gold-plated wrist watch and occasionally they still spent a Saturday night at the Palomino, if a group they liked was singing. Then his drinking got to be too much for her and she said her father had died of that shit and she was not going to put up with it in a husband.

When that marriage broke up, Ford sold all his clothes at a garage sale. The Oldsmobile station wagon went with the wife with the kids. He moved into a two story 'studio' on the beach at Malibu with his second wife. At 26, she was three years younger than his first wife, a small muscular woman with short curls, who worked as a secretary at Century City.

Their apartment was only 500 square feet, but the builder had cleverly engineered the vertical space to give a feeling of great spaciousness. The living room faced the ocean and had a two story wall of glass flanked by a fireplace in the corner. The kitchen and bath were at the inside wall of the long rectangular apartment, near the front door, and the bedroom was a loft over the kitchen, open to the living room from a balcony. Since the apartments were side by side with communal walls, neither the kitchen nor the bathroom had a window; the kitchen looked across the living room at the wall of glass. The most difficult adjustment Ford had to make was to the windowless bathroom, with its switch to activate a blower vent, which he found claustrophobic. The complex came with a Jacuzzi for the use of the 204 tenants, and Ford frequently used it late at night, when it was empty. He said it saved his sanity.

53

The second wife was into camping and Ford bought a Jeep Grand Cherokee Laredo 4-wheel drive. He acquired a beautiful set of expensive camping equipment, including air mattresses with foot bellows, nesting cooking equipment, all-weather sleeping bags, Coleman lanterns, and a bright blue snow tent made of parachute cloth. He started taking vitamin supplements because his wife complained he had no energy. On weekends he and his wife wore cutoff jeans, ripped across the legs. He wore a scuba diver's watch bought at Big Five Sporting Goods.

It was at this time that he first became hospitalized for his drinking, which led to the breakup of that marriage.

The camping stuff was easy to sell; there was apparently a good secondary market for it, including the scuba diving watch. The cutoff jeans, however, were discarded by his wife while he was at the hospital, immediately before she moved out, leaving a balance of two months' rent owing, and an eviction notice which screwed up his credit.

The third wife was nearly as tall as Ford; Jewish, slender, the daughter of a highly successful plastic surgeon. She was twenty three. Ford noted wryly that as he aged his wives got younger. This was the only marriage for which Ford went through a religious ceremony. He was married by a rabbi at the Century Park Hotel, the ceremony followed by a lavish dinner which was boycotted by her paternal grandparents because he was not an orthodox Jew.

The newlyweds rented a very posh two bedroom two bath apartment near Beverly Glen, and Ford became active in his wife's synagogue, explaining that although he was educated as a Catholic, his mother was Jewish and therefore, by Jewish law, so was he. The synagogue was sufficiently reformed so that Ford was taken at his word. He got a real estate license and started working between films for another actor-realtor in the synagogue.

I'm still trying, he thought at that time; I can still make it. He framed a motto for the wall of his bathroom, the smaller by far of the two bathrooms, which said, 'A man isn't finished when he's defeated, he's finished when he quits.'

Since this wife was a vegetarian, Ford became one, and they liked to drive to eat at places like The Good Earth. He sold the Jeep to pay the security deposit on a lease on a Lexus GS 300. A year after their marriage his wife presented him with a Patek Philippe wristwatch. Ford started to dress conservatively in lightweight wool suits and carefully understated sports clothes.

Ford actually liked this life and might have continued, but he noticed after the second year of marriage that his wife became more and more fearful. First she became afraid of travelling; then of being alone in the apartment; then she became convinced she was going to be the next victim of the Whistling Strangler, a serial killer then much in the newspapers. When he came home after a late night shoot, he would find her rigid with fear, hiding in the closet, her face covered with tears. No amount of remonstrating would comfort her, and after becoming hysterical because she claimed a man watched her when she threw out the garbage, she had to be hospitalized, after which Ford was again institutionalized for drinking. Her parents had her put in a conservatorship and served him in the drunk ward with divorce papers, which he did not contest.

Now he was a fervent member of Alcoholics Anonymous.

Having solved the drinking problem he discovered he now had an employment problem.

"I can't get you in anywhere," his agent said, eyes avoiding Ford, "Everybody in town says you're a drunk. Well, I don't know what you expected, after years of it."

So he was cast upon the mercy of Zoltan Diesel, who had hired him for Equity minimum, like some goddam extra. He needed to work, to be active. When he was active the depression diminished and he could avoid what came with it—the insomnia, the loss of appetite, the lethargy, the withdrawal from even trying to get roles. A bad mood seemed to color his judgment and he got fears about himself that didn't make sense at other times. But the damn chickenfeed salary from Diesel rankled; he was a better actor than Diesel was paying for, and he had spent years accumulating the knowledge Diesel was getting cheap.

"You know I'm a good actor, better than what you're paying for, and when the word gets around I'll have to start all over building my salary schedule. At least give me something," he begged Diesel, "a bonus when I finish the pilot, so everybody knows I'm dry."

"Look at it as a restart of your career."

"But you're not taking any risk if you pay me at the end."

"We both get something, Avery. I get a cheap male lead and you get a performance to point to when you're trying to convince the industry you're not still a drunk. If you're unhappy, Avery, I can replace you with Leon Sherman."

"Sherman?" Ford tilted his head. "You know I can say more with a hand gesture than that jerk can with forty five lines. The bonus would be small, an acknowledgment."

"I mean, candidly," Diesel's eyes were benign, "is there anybody else willing to hire you?"

So he had made the pilot for scale, and he was perfectly civil to Diesel, but he had this rage inside, inside somebody was stamping his little foot.

Ford was hurtling past his fortieth birthday. He didn't feel his body aging, but he kept at it, exercised every day. Still, he was constantly surprised by the little sags of aging he saw in himself. Somebody had taken color snapshots at a party recently and Ford was shocked to see the beginning of a double chin on the side of his face. He didn't see it yet when he looked full face in a mirror. In the morning he back-combed his hair at the temple and brushed it smooth to balance the jaw line, and checked his profile in the bathroom mirror with a hand mirror, looking at the chin.

And he found now he started to pee sometimes when he laughed. And he had seen June Allyson in a half minute TV spot pushing something called Depend, which turned out to be diapers for incontinent adults, which really depressed him.

Unmarried now, he bought a 77 MGB convertible, classic red, which was the apple of his eye. He discussed it with his shrink.

"Could be a healthy statement of vitality," the shrink said at last. The shrink rolled his shoulders, "Lack of fear for a new phase."

He figured he had maybe ten more years of male leads, and that was with luck. So, he had to get this pilot seen by the right people. His agent had written him off. It was a matter of pushing Diesel to aggressively market the pilot.

He and Boland were supposed to meet at Diesel's health club Thursday. He'd start on them then. He was going to be very close to that bastard, Diesel, and his flake, Boland. They were all going to be regular buddies. Until someday.

Chapter Seven

Zoltan Diesel, clad in a black one-piece zippered workout suit, pumped vigorously on an Exercycle at The Sporting Life, knees like pistons, eyes on the machine's counter.

The white Exercycles stood in rows of four, ten rows near the door of the gym; an Exercycle herd. The rest of the gym was full of twelve foot high rectangular pieces of weight equipment, enameled metallic blue, fitted with pulleys and metal cables and with chrome plated levers to control the amounts of weight.

The clicking of the machines was muted by wall to wall sisal mats. The room was immaculate, bathed in sunlight from three skylights, one wall mirrored, the other painted with brightly colored diagonal stripes. Beyond the striped wall was a lounge with couches and tables covered with the latest glossy magazines, and through a glass door on the other side of the room several men could be seen, eyes closed, head back, in a whirlpool bath.

"Zoltan, for Christ's sake, slow down. You're going to have a heart attack over those damn trees that got cut down and it's just not worth it," said a fat man wearing midnight blue polyester pants with piping that said Puma and a green tee shirt that strained to get across his breasts. He was astride a piece of weight equipment, pushing pudgy knees inward against black leather pads.

"I couldn't believe it, Walter. I mean, every single goddam tree. Those trees were prize winners."

"But Zoltan, I don't understand how it could have happened. Wasn't somebody at the house?" The fat man frowned sidewise at himself in the mirrors.

"Only the jerk houseboy. I canned him."

"Still, how--"

"Well, don't blame me." Avery Ford walked over, face and neck glistening with sweat, wearing loose gray sweatpants and a tee shirt. "I told that guy at your house something was wrong. Zoltan, I think somebody's mad at you."

"Avery, would you shut up?" Herb Boland was stomach-down over a bench, cautiously extending his calf muscles by bringing his heels to the floor, slowly, one at a time. "You don't know anything about it."

"People get mad, Herb; that's why you made the cast sneak out of Plonktown in the fucking middle of the night."

"What could I do about it? You think there was something I could do about it?"

"Herb, I work on some pretty ratty films, but by God the cast leaves by the light of day."

"When Zoltan called me in Plonktown to tell me there was a problem with the money, I had to get the crew out fast. Everybody up there has a gun. Those guys drive with rifle racks on the back windows of the pickups. You want to tell one of them he's not going to get paid?" Boland whined.

"You two rehash the same stuff," Diesel stopped pedaling. "It isn't as if anybody set out to screw those Plonktown people. It was just--"

"What?"

"--a cash flow problem. Trust me, my trees have nothing to do with Plonktown."

"Full range of motion, Mr. Hiller." A trainer with bulging muscles stopped beside the straining fat man. He carried a stack of thick folded white towels which emitted a fake lemony smell of detergent. "Leg all the way out, Mr. Hiller, then bring the knees in. No helping hands, there. Put your mind into the thigh muscle."

The fat man looked at the trainer and worked his knees faster.

Diesel pedaled. "What happened was, there was some kind of mix up; those meatballs were obviously supposed to clear one of my neighbor's places."

"Incredible," Walter said. "Where was the private guard? I mean, we pay for these guys."

"And that's not all; somebody broke into my garage the other night."

"Did I tell you what happened in my neighborhood?" Walter said.

"I have an alarm on the door of the Rolls because of the FAX and the telephone. Thank God, it must have scared them off."

"The burglaries in my neighborhood were a kid lived on the block." The fat man stopped pushing with his knees. "Nobody thought anything of him being around, so he had a nice thing going."

"And apparently they didn't even try to get into the Rolls."

"And the kid's parents are both psychologists and they told the rest of us they're having weekly family meetings to discuss the problem, which they say have been very candid. That's instead of slapping the kid upside the head."

"They didn't take anything in the garage, so obviously the alarm scared them off."

"These druggie kids just look for something they can sell easy. Little pricks."

"And I liked Plonktown." Ford said. "I figured I'd go back there for a couple of weeks. Not permanently, of course, I'm too much of a city rat. But for a sort of vacation."

"Oh Christ, please let's not start with Plonktown again. This is my exercise time." Diesel rolled his eyes.

"Fat chance of that now. People always blame the actors, because that's who they see." Ford stepped next to Walter, notched a slant board higher on the corner of one of the large rectangular pieces of weight equipment, hooked his feet under the stirrups, folded his arms across his chest, and started doing sit-ups up the slant board, head down. His upper abdominals visibly flexed as the sweat-soaked tee shirt clung to them. Walter stopped pressing with his knees again and watched Ford.

"They saw a lot of me too up in Plonktown, and I don't feel right about what went down with their checks." Boland said. "But nobody cut down Zoltan's trees because they're mad; that's ridiculous. You realize what they'd have to do to organize that? The trees were just some crazy fuckup. I don't believe in conspiracy theories; I believe in the fuckup theory."

"Herb, you have got to get back in control of the cast." Diesel flicked a glance at Avery. "The mark of the director has to be on every aspect of the production, so you get a coherent whole. Once you have actors going their own way, you might as well abdicate."

"Zoltan, I wish you hadn't taken that film course at U.C.L.A extension."

"This is not about film; this is about how you treat people." Avery said.

"I'll find out who ordered the service, of course." Diesel said. "I've got my girl calling around now. I think the route to go will be to sue the homeowner who ordered the service rather than the service itself. They're bound to have money if they live in my neighborhood. Although I'll make the service a party to the suit too."

"I haven't tightened up around the middle the way I should." The fat man patted the roll above his waist and grimaced in the mirror. "I feel terrible all the time and there doesn't seem to be a thing I can do about it. I think I may need to hire a personal trainer."

"You need to stress the muscle." Avery Ford panted. "You see people been working three months, three times a week, and they don't look any different. Because when they started they had a trainer explain to them how to do the simplest thing, and they never take the pin out of the first hole, so there's no stress on the muscle. You need that stress."

"What are you doing here?" Walter's pin was in the first hole. "You don't even look fat."

"I am fighting encroaching decay. Like most out-of-work actors, I have to come to a place like this when I'm invited." Ford went back to his sit-ups. "Because I can't afford it. Which is the same reason you see actors making sandwiches out of the hors d'oeuvres at parties."

"I still can't believe the crew would be that dumb." Diesel said. "They were obviously valuable trees."

"Oh, listen, workmen today—I could tell you stories." Walter said.

"Your looks are something you have to maintain in this biz." Ford said.

"I devoted all day yesterday to looking up tree law." Diesel said, "And I've really got them. Turns out the statutory laws concerning trees are codified under the civil code going back to 1886. There were five major tree cutting cases decided right here in California. There are some marvelous precedents."

"Zoltan, forget the trees." Boland said. "When I picked up Avery, he's got a Murphy bed in that place of his over on Bronson. I've always wanted to do one of those great comic Murphy bed routines."

"Don't start. I hate that damned bed." Ford stopped his sit-ups again. "I'm afraid to move when I'm in it. I'm afraid to get out of it at night to pee. Thank God I haven't got a woman at the moment, I'd be afraid we'd both get folded up in our raptures."

"I don't want simple trespass. The damages will be in proving the value of the trees." Diesel nodded as he pedaled. "I'm getting a professional survey of the property showing where each one was located. And I'm having the place re-fertilized and replanted."

"Now, I see a Murphy bed sequence as part of a serious film." Boland stopped stretching, his eyes distant. "A quick dream sequence, but funny—really funny, very Dennis Potter. Did you see 'The Singing Detective?' "

"I had a bit of luck. My girl found a study some outfit in Visalia did of the value of trees—how much more home buyers will pay for a home on a property with plenty of trees. Wooded lots in new subdivisions sell for thousands more than treeless ones, and some developers figure fifteen percent more for the same house surrounded by trees. So I get the property appraised and then go after the fifteen percent. Which should be sizeable."

"Zoltan, so you'll just replace the trees." Ford said.

"That is exactly what I won't do—I will not just replace the trees. I have to hand-select each of the new trees. It's a tremendous amount of time away from the office, over and above the economic loss of the trees themselves."

"But you need to market the pilot. You need to focus on what's important." Ford went back to his sit-ups. "If you get distracted, who's going to market the pilot? We don't want to bury the pilot, that was some creative work."

"And, of course, organizing the money for the new western we're going to do is itself a creative act." Diesel revolved his wrist watch to the bone of his wrist and started taking his working heart rate.

"Separating people from their money is a creative act?" Ford asked.

"You guys can act or direct or whatever, but no money means nobody sees what you do. So in many ways, yes, organizing the money is the most creative part of the project, the linchpin that makes it all work." Reminded, Diesel pushed in the pin on his watch.

"Which means you convince some plumbing contractor he's part of a movie if he pays for twenty per cent of the action."

"We facilitate his being part of a creative act, yes. You've never understood the importance of that, Avery, which is why I emphasize how important it is you stop complaining about the Plonktown pilot. Yes, our investors dream a little. We aren't where we are today because we mock their dreams. Now can we go on to something else?"

"What's your working heart rate?" Ford asked.

"150," Diesel smirked. "Not bad."

"Mine's 130."

"Every tree has to be right for the microenvironment it's going in." Diesel went back to pedaling. "And I'm the only person who knows what's grown well before and where. Of course, the new trees will be saplings—mine were mature trees. Goddam, I miss my trees. Seeing them was the positive wave in my day."

"Avery, maybe I could get you some money to let us use that Murphy bed." Boland walked over and stood by Ford. "In fact, your whole apartment would be a great downscale set—all those plastic chairs and the aluminum sliding doors; it has this terrific ratty look."

"I'm in that apartment temporary." Ford's lips closed in a stubborn line. "Just until I get things back together in my career."

"That's why I said I'd take you over after we finish today, introduce you to the guy who's casting the new western I'm starting for Zoltan. There's a great role in it. Older cowboy, seen it all, amused by the kids he works with but still can show the kids a trick or two. A lanky, patrician gunslinger."

"Really?" Avery put on a brooding, far-off look. He withdrew his tongue to the back of his mouth and separated his lips to look parched. Somehow he lengthened the space between his ribcage and his hip bones. He became the gunslinger.

"Sure, there you go, that role is you."

"You can't say Bronson Avenue if the casting guy asks where I live." Ford grabbed Boland's arm. "Give him my agent's number. You start off wrong with these guys if they think you don't live in a successful nabe."

"Relax, I already talked to him about you for this role."

"Because I'm beginning to sound like these actors with upferitis you see 11 o'clock every morning at Starbucks. You know, I'm up for this; I'm up for that."

"You're sweating this role and you don't have to." Boland put one of the lemony towels around his shoulders. "I told you, you're in."

"The main advantage of my apartment on Bronson is it's got underground parking, which keeps the MG off the streets." Ford returned the slant board to its usual position.

"Didn't I see you on TV last week?" Walter said. "You were--"

"Probably. Lately my stuff seems to be all over the tube, but the powers that be in Hollywood won't give me a job because I'm a recovering alcoholic."

"Really? I don't see how you could make all those movies if you were a drunk." Walter stopped pressing his knees and gingerly balanced on the weight equipment, feet out in a vee.

"When I was a drunk they gave me work. It's now I'm sober they won't." Ford grunted, back to the sit-ups, this time on the floor. "I'm a much better actor than I was before."

"Not that any of this is going to compensate me for the emotional loss. I'll never forget coming home and finding the whole place chopped down." Diesel shifted gears on the Exercycle. "I could easily have some kind of psychological problem. I'd better start seeing somebody—remind me to look up who's an experienced man to testify."

"Or the other way I might go," Walter was pushing in on the knee pads again, "is isometric exercises. Frank says those isometric exercises isolate and sculpt specific muscle groups and you get faster results."

"We could play some racquetball." Diesel waved toward the court.

"You really want to kill me?" Walter swung his leg back to one side and sat on his machine. "You've got this shot drops in the corner, there's no way to return it. You play racquetball like other people play war games."

"And I'm going to have a conservatory put on the back of the house," Diesel said, "for the young plants. I can justify that expense to the court."

"See? So you may come out of this with something positive." Walter said.

"And then they gave me a hand." Diesel said.

"A HAND?" Walter snapped his knees closed. "Zoltan, that's sick!"

"Not a real hand, a hand, you know, made of some kind of white plastic. I think it's part of a garden sculpture."

"Wait a minute, I didn't see that." Ford said. "That's interesting. I was in a movie once where a guy had all these parts of bodies he killed, kept them in a kind of museum."

"I don't see why anybody would be in a movie like that." Walter chided. "God knows, there are enough crazies out there without giving them more ideas."

"I try to make sure if it's a role I don't like, that it makes me a lot of money." Ford said. He sat up from the slant board and gently massaged his upper abdominals.

"And the police seem to have no idea where to begin." Diesel said.

"Oh, the police, everybody knows what they're doing." Walter said. "They're dragging their heels until the ballot initiative in April. They want more tax money, on our property taxes of course. What, people who don't own property don't use the police?"

"They don't seem to regard the sawing down of trees as important. I had to insist they make a full report for the insurance. Not that they'll give me anything like the replacement value of those trees." Diesel started on the Exercycle again.

"I don't understand what it is with insurance." Walter said. "Other people make money from insurance, but I never do. It's really all your agent."

"Still, Zoltan, we need you out marketing the Plonktown pilot. You can't get distracted with your trees." Boland said.

"Zoltan, for God's sake," Walter said. "I can't even watch you. You make me sick; your face is all red. I tell you, illness is the big stick—it gets your attention. You better start thinking about your blood pressure. You should come to my meditation class."

"What meditation class?" Ford asked. "Maybe that would be good for me."

"It's really terrific." Walter said. "You know, lots of things you think relax you really don't. Those guys sitting in that tub for instance," Walter nodded at the whirlpool—"are doing nothing, believe me, nothing. Meditation, that's what gets the blood pressure down."

Diesel got off the Exercycle, accepted a towel from the attendant, and started for the door with a casual wave.

"What about the Greek place in Westwood for lunch?" Walter hurried to follow Diesel out. "I heard at court they make great stuffed dolma."

"You finished?" Boland asked Ford. "This is eye-glazing boring."

"Okay. You ready for a shvitz?"

"Sure." Boland said.

"Then we'll go see that casting guy. I don't want his attention to wander."

In the steam room, where most men opened like starfish, Boland sat on the lowest shelf with his knees crossed, foot bouncing, his back curved, one elbow propped on the bench above him, a coiled spring. Ford extended prone on the very top wooden shelf, open and sweating. "You'll keep after Diesel about the Plonktown pilot being seen?"

"Yeah." Boland said. "Now he's writing some book on attack negotiating or whatever it is he calls what he does."

"He should call it 'Weasel's Guide to Wheeler Dealing'."

"I want you in the western because you're good and you work cheap and as long as it's cheap, Diesel will do it. Cheap is what he's into."

"Thanks, Herb, for that." Ford flopped over. "Anyway, no more. I told my agent—one time I worked for minimum, just to show people I'm dry. From here on in I get feature player."

"Bastard Diesel, I just can't get him to shut up about the damn trees, and now he's starting about a book." Boland wiped his face from the steam.

"You heard that, right, Herb? I want feature player and a negotiated credits position. You want me because I'm good. Period."

"Avery, you go along to get along in this business."

"Because whether it's the drinking or just me, I find I have no friends, just people I work with. So I have to take care of my work, because that's all I've got."

"Diesel should of got the finger, not the hand." Boland said.

Avery Ford sat up so abruptly he cracked his head on the cedar ceiling. "That hand—Jesus Christ, Herb, the hand! I know who cut down Zoltan's trees!"

"Then for God's sake," Boland got up off his bench, "tell me."

Chapter Eight

Sally Richard first met Henry Ponziano Richard when she walked into his furniture store on Plonktown's plaza, offering to sketch the merchandise for ads, which is how she supported herself as an art major at Humboldt State University.

The early residents of Plonktown came north for the gold and stayed for the lumber. Built in the 1850's as a landing to float logs down Humboldt Bay to the sawmills at Samoa, Plonktown still had a line of two story brick commercial buildings that fronted the expansive plaza. These buildings originally housed the great mercantile establishments that lined the plaza and sent supplies to the miners and loggers by mule train. Since Plonktown lacked a deepwater port, a railroad spur was constructed for the merchants from two hundred feet out in the bay to a depot at the Southwest corner of the plaza, where the merchants received their goods and brought them to buildings which were commercial stores on the main floor and storage space on the second.

The survival of these buildings was peculiar in California, where old buildings are routinely demolished in the name of progress. But in Plonktown, where the economy was stagnant, there was little call for the wrecker's ball. As a result, the current resident strolling in the plaza could see the high hopes and disappointments of past commercial ventures fixed in the still visible names in the brick facades and octagonal tile entrances of the stores. Henry had bought a building which dated from 1872.

Sally was 23 at the time, and Henry was 45. In a town where people dressed like a full page from the L.L.Bean catalog, Sally stood out like an exotic bird. Beneath her ash blond boy's haircut, four inch black hoop earrings dangled from silver hooks through her ear lobes. Her blouse was a mustard and black tiger print, and she wore opaque panty hose ending in black patent flat heel oxfords. Her black wool mini skirt cleared her crotch by an inch and clung like a sweater to her high buttocks. The day she met Henry she wore peach eye shadow.

In Henry she saw a man with glasses, a balding pate surrounded by stringy hair, and pants legs that broke wrong at the instep of his shoes and dragged at the heels of his short legs. He listened to her pitch and then began to go through some acrylic sketches she had made of the furniture in his window. The other merchants made a decision after looking at two or three sketches, but Henry looked at all the sketches.

"I like your colors," he said.

"Thank you."

"Reminds me of an artist named Egon Schiele."

"You know Egon Shiele?" She realized how that sounded and made a stab at recovery, "What I mean is, not many people around here know about him."

"I like the German Expressionists," he said. "I used to try to copy Shiele's style of portraits, those awkward postures, like sitting on the floor with one leg extended. I was an art major in college."

As he talked, Henry's face became animated. To her amazement, he had an encyclopedic knowledge of art. They started to talk about artists they both liked. Then they talked about artists they both hated. Then they wound up laughing uproariously together at some of the recent posturings of the New York school. After about an hour he offered to take her to dinner that evening and show her his paintings.

Sally had been a stewardess for three years earning enough money to return to college. She cheerfully assumed he was on the make, but a dinner was a dinner. Back in her room she hesitated over what to wear. Dinner could mean the McDonald's on Highway 101. What the hell, she thought, it was nice of him to ask.

She selected the prettier of her two dresses, a thin, flowered turquoise cotton with long sleeves and a full skirt that came down to her shins and showed off her slender waist. She wore her Navajo earrings, small pieces of turquoise embedded in silver studs and dangling small silver arrows. When she saw him she was glad she had dressed up.

He'd gone home to change to a dark blue suit. And a vest. He looked funereal.

He took her to The Gallant Frog, a country restaurant which a young couple had opened in a former grocery store about twenty miles up the coast from the University. The man cooked; the woman seated patrons; there were fresh flowers and white linens on the tables and harp music on the stereo speakers.

"A local secret." Henry said, pleased with her delight, "Because nobody can find this place." The woman seemed to know and like Henry, and shot Sally curious sidewise glances. They started with a duck sausage and local sliced tomatoes with a rectangular homemade bread served on a little cutting board.

"They have a bunch of signature breweries up here," Henry ordered some bottles of local beer. "Where one man makes a small amount of beer each year," he explained to her questioning look. "They can fiddle around with the hops and the timing. Some are very good. Red Tail Ale is one of the best."

"This crab is fantastic," she said, when the main course arrived. "I never knew it could be this good."

"It's because it's real fresh," Henry said. "Caught this morning. They buy it off the fishing boat on Woodley Island." They finished with a torte made with bittersweet chocolate.

She glanced at Henry's unimpressive figure, the dark polyester suit, the awkward movements.

"You surprise me, how much you know about a lot of things." She said.

"Comes from being devoted to my stomach," he patted it, "and beginning to look it."

And then he took her to his house.

The original part of Henry's house was small, built next to the river, and made of wood from the surrounding redwood forest. A flight of wood steps rose from a flat parking pad covered with pebbles to a deck outside a wide front door, also made of redwood. The place had the lush smell of the forest. And the quiet. The only sound was the river.

"I need a wall around that parking pad," he pointed, "to keep out the duff."

She looked where he was pointing.

"The leaves," he pointed. "I've been meaning to get to it."

At the rear of the house was a second taller structure, also built from redwood, which had the same shape as the house, and consisted of one large sky lit room with a full bath and a broad deck which ran along the river. Henry had furnished the deck with the best line of patio furniture from his store, but the only furniture in the large room was a storage area of vertical wooden slots Henry had constructed along one wall, to hold his finished canvasses.

"What a great place." Sally looked around. "How long have you had it?"

"My dad built the original house. He loved it here. Of course it was much smaller then. I added the big room in back. He wasn't here all that much; he was a musician, played in bands, pickup bands all around the state. He changed our name from Ricciardi to Richard, said it was easier in the bands." He stopped. "I'm talking too much."

Sally had learned to keep a conversation going during her days as a stewardess. Within an hour she knew more about Henry than most people who grew up with him.

"So you put on the extra room so you could paint--"

"Not exactly. It was for my brother's kids."

"They lived here?"

"When my mom got sick, my dad bought a mobile home in a park down in Hemet in the desert, because it was too damp for her up here. My older brother, Tony, had been married twice, and he had three kids."

"And so they came here?"

"Well, all the time I'd be getting phone calls from my mom, saying 'your brother needs you to wire him some money' or 'your brother's kid is sick and what are you going to do about it?'

"I don't see why it was you—"

71

"Anyway, he plays in bands too, like my dad, so he brought the kids down there, to Hemet. It was the only place. But the mobile home park had an adults only rule."

"So then you brought the kids here?"

"My parents brought the kids here. I was living in the house after they left for Hemet, and I'd started the store. I had some money, so I added the room in the back and the kids lived back there. My parents lived into their eighties. They died about three years ago." He grinned. "Good stock, we are."

"Where are the kids now?"

"Well, Tony was going with a stewardess named Sandra at the time." Henry was sliding out paintings and leaning them against the walls to be seen. "A nice girl, about half his age. Anyway, she got pregnant. So he married her, and then he thought, since he was going to have a house with her, he might as well get everybody together."

"Do you get to see the kids?"

"Well, they're teenagers now, and they have their own lives." His voice trailed off.

"Still, I'd think--"

"I sent them the money and they're coming this summer." He brightened.

"I see."

"Well, don't say it that way. They all get along real well. Everybody gets along with Tony, even his two ex-wives."

"I see."

"Why do you keep saying that?"

"Nervous habit."

"Anyway, I had the space, and I was an art major in college, like I said, so after they left I decided to go back to painting. Been away from it for years, so it took me a while to get what I want down."

"Did you show these paintings at your store?"

"I haven't shown them to anybody yet. Be careful," he said, "I'm feeling sort of fragile about them."

To her surprise, he displayed fourteen photo-realistic paintings, in wild fauve colors, each one carefully worked. Obviously, this was a body of several years' work. She took over a half hour to go through them. Then she arranged them in three groups. Then she sat in front of one of the groups.

"Henry, have you ever tried anything—well, looser? More like the impressionists? Like these over here?" She pointed to the group in front of her.

"That's what I'm trying to do now."

"This one," she picked one up, "is much more—well, punchy."

"That's the last one I did." He smiled broadly. "How great, you zeroed right in on it. That's the direction I'm trying to go."

Sally walked back into the main room of the original house. A river stone fireplace dominated the room, and Henry made a fire to keep out the forest chill. On the mantle were photographs of three teenagers, one smiling in high school graduation robes.

She settled on the rug in front of the fireplace, long legs toward the fireplace, leaning back on one elbow. She extended and circled one foot.

"My family's not close," she said. "Tony's kids are lucky. I mean; not just him, but you, and their grandparents."

"Italian families are like that. You don't get away from them."

Silence.

"I feel awkward as a kid with you. And I can smell your perfume. And I figure I'm about twenty years older than you, and I feel ridiculous."

"Why don't you just sit down?" she pointed on the rug next to her.

"Brandy?" He took out a decanter. "They're making brandy up here now. In Ukiah."

She sipped the brandy and looked at him across the cut crystal.

"I'm driving to the Bay Area next weekend," she said. "They have the Vienna 1900 show in from New York; it's at the De Young. Supposed to be great."

"They've got three Schieles never been in this country," she continued. "And they have a great old glass and iron front from one of the Paris Metro stations."

Silence.

"Come with me?"

He put down his glass. "I'd have to close the store on a Saturday."

"Put up a sign. Say you're on a buying trip. Tell them to stop back, because the new stuff will be sold, 'First come, first served'."

And then Henry surprised her again.

"Why do you want me to come? You're so pretty. I don't think I'm any great stud."

"I know all about studs." She tilted her head. "Pecker erectus maximus."

"WHAT?" he asked, aghast.

"I already had what you could call my testosterone phase and once it's done, it's done. I don't need to do it again. Like Picasso's blue period. I'd really like it if you'd come to the Bay Area. It would be fun."

Within 3 months they were married. It was the kind of marriage of which people said, "They're a strange couple." Her friends said she was looking for a meal ticket. His friends said he was looking to get laid. Neither set of friends could pass an evening without some pointed remark, so Henry and Sally wound up spending a lot of time alone together.

Which was fine.

The first summer the kids came to visit him. She prepared a dinner for them, which they ate enthusiastically.

"Uncle Henry," said Tony Junior, the middle boy, "can we have the car? We're going into town."

"Can we have a couple of bucks?" said Mark, the oldest boy.

"I think Uncle Henry would like it if you would build a wall around the parking area." Sally said.

"What?" Mark said.

"What the hell are we supposed to build a wall with?" Tony Junior said.

"There are plenty of stones in the river." Sally said. "You have to fit them in, though. You can start tomorrow."

"Jesus," Tony Junior said.

"And before you go," she said to Tony Junior, "would you clear away the dishes?"

"Ha." Mark said.

"You can wash," she said to Mark, "And you can dry and put away," to Catherine, the youngest girl.

Behind her back Tony Junior made a face.

Mark started to run water, splashing loudly in the kitchen sink. "You're supposed to be scraping the dishes before you give them to me," he accused Tony Junior.

"How am I supposed to know where to put the stuff all over them?"

"Just take them to the garbage and scrape them. What am I supposed to do with dishes with food all over them?"

"Oh, just like always, you wash one dish and suddenly you're an expert."

"Wait a minute," Mark said to Catherine, "where do you think you're going?"

"I have to pee."

"Oh no, you don't. Nobody goes until we finish."

"But I have to go—"

"We know all about it. You stay here and wipe."

"But I don't know where anything goes--"she whined.

"So, dummy, open the cabinet and look for the same plate. You always do this; you figure if you act stupid enough and make people keep telling you the same thing, they'll get disgusted and you'll get out of the work."

"Oh boy, I'm glad you're taking a course in psychology in college--"

"I'm going to slap you upside the head with this frying pan--"

"I better go see." Henry said, getting up from a chair on the deck.

"Sit down." Sally firmly pushed him back down.

"But he'll hit her; she's a girl--"

"It'll be fine." Sally said. "The last time my brother hit me, I was fifteen. I stole his car keys and didn't give them back until he swore never to hit me again, ever. Took two days."

"You don't think I should just—"

"We'll be on the deck." She called to the kids. "Watching the river."

The next day the kids started on the parking wall.

Two months later Sally persuaded Henry a visit to Las Vegas would be fun. He called his brother, Tony, and informed him they'd be staying a few days. Tony didn't look like Henry; he was tall and rangy with a flashing grin. After Tony got over his initial shock, he found he actually enjoyed his unaccustomed role as host, and he played it to the hilt, including barbecuing a dinner for them in his back yard and expounding on the merits of hickory vs. mesquite for grilling.

After three days Tony discreetly hit on Sally when he was alone with her, and was firmly, courteously rejected. He seemed relieved. By the time they left, Tony was introducing Sally as his sexy new sister-in-law, and commenting that there was more to old Henry than appearances, because he'd picked himself off a lovely.

Sally and Henry had been married now for five years. She convinced him his clothes should be more on the cutting edge of style; that the store would benefit. He took his slacks to a tailor in Eureka, who cut the pants length correctly, and she bought him shirts in deep blues and eggplant purple. She lightened his tendency to fuss, and he provided something she had never had—an anchor.

At the store Sally put in a line of Kosta Boda glass, each piece numbered in the glass on the bottom, and a line of wood serving spoons which a local craftsman had carved to follow the sinuous curve of the yew. She got a group of hand-woven angora throws in soft heather colors, which she draped across two upholstered chairs with a sign in Italic script, "For those cool Humboldt evenings." People started to stop by after the farmers market to see what was new and Henry's store became the place to go when you wanted something special.

And Henry turned out to have a talent for acquiring real estate. Which is what he did with the extra money from the second trust deed he put on the store; the money he expected to get back from the film company. Of course, it was going to be very tight now, with two notes to pay on the store building. Plus, he didn't have the money to fix up the second building and get tenants in it. But it would all work itself out. Henry had confidence.

Chapter Nine

Yancey Harly stared at the screen of his Amiga computer, which he had set up for blue letters against a red background, and delicately browsed within the list of Nebula Films phone numbers he'd gotten from Marge.

He was wearing dark blue flannel PJ's printed with surf boards because it was cold; wrapped in a tan Pendleton blanket, with his feet in unbleached wool socks hooked around the legs of his secretary chair, and the only light in the room was the glow of the screen. He was using the modem to try to sign on to the Nebula Films system. He was guessing the correct passwords for Nebula's residual accounting software. That is, his predictable password program was guessing.

He had no way of knowing the particular password to get into the file that paid residuals, but most people were not too creative with the passwords they used as security locks on simple computer files. Nebula would have fancy security on any program that actually paid money; but internal accounting records would have a low level of protection because there would be no reason for anybody to break into them, and anything harder would make it harder to use. People forgot fancy passwords.

Yancey bit his tongue delicately and leaned forward, concentrating. He frowned slightly. His posture was terrible. He was freezing, and his father would have a fit if he walked in the room. But his father wouldn't walk in, because it was 3 A.M.

Yancey had set his alarm to try to use his new predictable password program in the middle of the night, when he figured there was less chance of someone using an accounting program at Nebula and noticing the activity. It was just as well, because his father tended to get hyper about things like this.

Just to be sure, Yancey typed in an instruction before putting in the program that any replies were to be sent to a number he had found on Marge's list of phone numbers at the University of California at Santa Cruz. Anybody finding his program, which was not likely to begin with, would figure the program originated at Santa Cruz.

Yancey opened his shoebox and removed a disc, inserting it into a drive and booting up a new program which had a well-chosen list of 1600 predictable passwords, to try to discover the encrypted password at Nebula. 'A' was for alphabet, American, Apollo, Axis, etc. The program was also set up to produce such frequently used passwords as common first names; every date after January 1, 1960—which would include the birth dates of most programmers—and the word 'hello'. The program would try the passwords in lightning sequence.

He'd gotten the predictable password program off an electronic bulletin board. The bulletin boards were a system of free exchange which had operated wildly for years, until the government started taking a dim view of the information given away on them. In 1986 Congress passed the Computer Fraud and Abuse Act, which, among other things, made it a crime to gain unauthorized entry into a computer. That didn't stop the electronic bulletin boards. Eavesdropping was easy to accomplish and difficult to detect, making the law difficult to administer. But the descriptions of programs on the electronic bulletin boards became a lot more oblique after the law was passed.

For Yancey's program, some guy down in Marin had spent all his evenings for weeks trying every word in the dictionary to see which words actually got him into other people's programs, and then produced the computer instructions for a predictable password program, as an experiment. The program didn't erase any files and it wasn't designed to be destructive. The guy in Marin put hours of labor into making the list, not counting his telephone bill, and then gave it away free, because the fun was in making the program, and he believed all information belonged to the world. The aim was technical prowess; a thumbing of the nose at computer fences, not vandalism.

All of this seemed eminently reasonable to Yancey. In fact, he was rapt with admiration for the guy in Marin.

The electronic bulletin boards also posted free-wheeling personal ads, and Tom Harly would have been amazed to learn Yancey was posting computer mash notes, on which his tag was 'Horny from Humboldt'.

From the corner of his eye, Yancey glimpsed a yellow movement on the floor. "Damn," he muttered. He used the front cover of a manual to scoop up a five inch long bright yellow banana slug. Then he pattered through the house; opened the kitchen door; and gently deposited the slug outside among the soaked leaves.

Marge was a pretty good female, but she did get upset by banana slugs. She'd be running around putting salt around all the floor furnace openings. Yancey didn't want her to kill the slug by drying it up with salt. He liked banana slugs because they had no camouflage and no defenses. And he read somewhere that they had a really kinky sex life. They were hermaphrodites; and they bit each other as part of mating and sometimes hunks of flesh got bitten off. And that left the right side of each slug battered and scarred.

And then often they got stuck in each other during sex and had a helluva time getting back out. Sometimes they were found dead, clasped. Interesting.

He reminded himself of banana slugs when he thought his problems were terrible. Like, there was this girl at school and she was crazy about purple, always wore purple stuff, and he had tried to talk to her, genuinely tried. He told her he could make her screen purple. In the computer lab. And she had looked at him like he wasn't even speaking English.

And his mom had made a remark about him spending his school breaks when he was at M.I.T. with her. Shit. He'd need a cover story that didn't hurt her feelings. Maybe say he was visiting a friend, except that would require a complicated series of lies. He didn't have a friend at school now; seemed unlikely he'd have one at M.I.T. If he got a job in one of the computer labs, he'd tell her he had to work vacations.

He went back to his computer screen. Yancey fervently hoped the Nebula programmer hadn't used some goddam nonsense word as a password for his 'back door'; the secret way the programmer could easily gain access to fine-tune the program. If Yancey found the password everything would be fine. A nonsense word would screw Yancey up because there was no way of guessing it. But accounting offices generally didn't use nonsense words because such words seemed beneath the dignity of the serious business being transacted. And a lot of programmers just used their birth dates or a mother's maiden name as passwords.

Yancey continued the program and opened eight of the files within the system which turned out to have passwords on the predictable list. He scrolled them, examining the stored information; but they didn't seem to be what he wanted. He stopped and blinked his eyes. His eyes started burning when he stared at the screen with his damn glasses on, and he couldn't read the screen with them off.

It was with the ninth list he got lucky and found Herb Boland listed. The password was Sesame. Some goddam creative type figured that one out.

What he seemed to be looking at was a simple tally of Boland's film work which had been screened during the month, plus any extras, with a total residual figure at the bottom.

Yancey considered. He could add some names to the list, but he didn't know which of Boland's works were likely to be in circulation, and he risked coming up with something that would attract Boland's attention. If he left the list but changed the total, the figures listed wouldn't add up to the total on the bottom. That would only work if Boland just looked at the total.

Would Boland be likely to just look at the total? He got a statement every month, and when he was in Plonktown, the guy always seemed to be in a rush.

It was a judgment call. Yancey closed his eyes. Better to multiply each figure by a constant. A list of numbers that did not add up was just too easy to detect. He issued the instruction to add an extra zero to each film's earnings and then to the month's statement total, and then brought the statement back up.

He looked with pride at the statement Boland would receive. Looked just fine to him.

Outstanding! He hadn't been all that sure the predictable password program would actually work. He would celebrate, he decided. The ice cream store on the plaza in Plonktown had a new sundae they called The Garbage Pail. He hadn't had one because he was watching the old weight.

The day after Thanksgiving, no school. He'd have one then, he promised himself. This Friday.

Chapter Ten

Venice, California, was built by Abbot Kinney, a dreamer and heir to the Sweet Caporal cigarette fortune, who came to the Pacific Ocean for his respiratory ailments in the first part of the 20th century and decided to reproduce the Italian city on the mudflats of Southern California. Not just as any city, mind, but "an upper middle-brow Italianate Chautauqua resort."

In 1905 he dug a system of canals; put in moon bridges; and created an area of two story commercial buildings with Moorish arches, lacy plaster exteriors, and covered sidewalk arcades, and opened Venice of America. He rented tents to the summer tourists who flocked to see the waterside lots he had for sale. Along the canals, he built small wood frame houses, and he created a grid of two-block-long walk streets, closed to vehicle traffic, running at right angles to the ocean, with names like Breeze and Wavecrest, where he put large two story wood frame houses.

With time, the canals silted in and oil companies killed the area for residential use by festooning it with working oil rigs, fouling air and water, and hastening the waterways' decline. Mornings you could smell the canals from the dead fish. The beats arrived in the 60's to live in the cheap rents and continue a tradition of Venice as a center for the creative. Something about being next to the water; something about the way the light glanced off the waves, made people see things different.

The statewide real estate boom of the 70's brought in a new crop of owners with greater expectations—artists, musicians, filmmakers, and the affluhip investors who followed close behind them. Some houses sold three times in one year.

The new residents passed environmental restrictions to shove the oil companies off the beach and Venice became one of the few areas of Los Angeles that was urban, in that 80-year-old ramshackle houses stood immediately next to townhouses with 'gee whiz' architecture and monthly rents in the four figures.

The long-term tenant who used to live in Herb Boland's apartment was kicked out by rising rent and wound up collecting signatures on Ocean Front Walk, first for an initiative for rent control, and later for an ordinance limiting home sale prices in the beach zone. His problem, Herb said, was that he invested in the stock market, which went down, instead of the housing market, which went up.

Herb Boland's apartment took up the ground floor of what had been a two story one family house on a Venice walk street, a block and a half from the ocean. He set up a file cabinet and desk for his computer on what used to be a rear service porch. Above the computer he put a bulletin board covered with notes to himself. The original dining room held a glass-topped verdigris metal coffee table in front of a rattan couch with 1920's flowered print, a mission oak hassock with the same print, and a dhurrie rug, and a wood burning fireplace faced with stream-rounded boulders. The fireplace was why Boland rented the apartment and it made up, in his mind, for the inconvenience of having to sleep in the glassed-in front porch.

The entire apartment had walls and ceilings made of narrow batten board redwood strips, painted many times, currently a pale green. Boland was fond of telling colleagues that he got in a bathing suit on Friday at 6 P.M. and stayed in bathing suits until Monday. Now, dressed in an old bathing suit, a sweatshirt, and a pair of Mexican huaraches, Boland collapsed in front of his computer, booted up a word processing program, and started to rip open his mail with the tip of a large knife curved like a scimitar.

"Herb, we have got to get some decent blinds," Stacy Wade came in from the sleeping porch. "I was getting out of bed and some guy stopped in the walk way and stood there staring. With his mouth open."

"Well, you're worth staring at. Even with his mouth open."

"Honey, did my registration date for Santa Monica College come in?" She gestured to the mail.

"Goddam," he said, "nothing but junk mail. More Christmas catalogs." He flipped through one. "Where the

84

hell do they find these backgrounds? They've gotta have the world's best location man. Models always look like they're photographed in some 14th Century French courtyard. Look at this one, she's wearing a coachman's hat and a greatcoat. Can't you just see that in L.A?"

"Just throw that stuff out." Stacy said. "I don't buy from catalogs. I like to try stuff on."

"I was hoping Jax Davis would get back to me on that western script. I gotta get the script firmed up because Zoltan is talking he may want to do some of the writing. Says he wants to be more hands-on the creative stuff. So if I get it firmed up and he pays for it, he's cheap enough so I can talk him into waiting for the next film to screw around with the script." He hooked a metal wastebasket with his foot and screeched it across the floor close to him, then dropped in several thick catalogs with a clang.

"Herb, that's just silly," she said. "You're the writer. Tell him no."

"Zoltan doesn't do no," Herb said. "It's not in his frame of reference."

"I better get an early registration this time. I want to get in that ceramic sculpture course and the damn thing always fills up right away."

"Nope." He fingered through the rest of the mail. "Didn't come in."

"Damn!" Stacy put her hands on her hips, tall, tan, blond hair pulled to the top of her head, a few wisps escaping. "Maybe I could get the teacher to give me an add card. I don't see why I always get late registration. It's bad enough they let people from Santa Monica register first."

"Stace, how long you been going to that place?" He tilted back on the chair.

"Pico Tech? That's what the students call it. Years."

"You never get any kind of degree? I worry about your head. Course, the rest of you is good enough so--" he wiggled his eyebrows.

"I'm not going for a degree. I like going. Everybody I know goes there."

He was still leafing through the mail, tossing each piece into the wastebasket with a satisfying thunk. "I must be on every clothing catalog list in the Western Hemisphere. Between that and the real estate pitches, I'm going to open the mail over the outside garbage can, wastebasket's not big enough."

"You know the real estate guys? They've started giving out flyers on Ocean Front Walk too. You ought to think about buying something, Herb."

"I have been thinking about it," he said. "Look at this; it's a computer printout of all the beach property sold for ten blocks north and south. Some real estate guy sent it to me. They're getting some amazing prices." He reached for a bowl of potato chips stationed on top of the file cabinet.

"That's what I mean," Stacy took away the bowl. "If we're gonna get something, we better do it now."

He crunched the one large chip he had snatched.

"Herb, you don't listen to what your body is telling you. You run around, you get yourself overtired and then you eat all that salty crap, like those potato chips. You know that salt holds water. I mean, I take you to the farmer's market on Fridays with me, but you never eat a vegetable."

"Well I can't eat those rice cakes you're always eating. Things look like the Styrofoam box they come in and taste like it too."

"I could slice you some cukes."

"I—that's funny," he said.

"What?" she swept the wisps of her hair up with her right hand.

"Look at this; the statement from Nebula looks pretty good. Zoltan was talking that if we brought in the Plonktown pilot at budget, there'd be a nice bonus. Anyway, I'll have to give him a ring—he apparently swung the bonus."

"Honey," she squealed, "how neat!"

"Well, it's nice to know the studio appreciates. For a while there, I was kind of upset at what we did to those people in that town."

"Hey, you can't make an omelet without breaking eggs," she intoned and then selected an emery board and started working on a fingernail.

"Maybe I won't call him. Right now I don't need Zoltan getting started on how wonderful he is. I'm seeing him tomorrow anyway. Avery Ford insists he's got some idea about the people cut down Zoltan's trees."

"Shhh. I need to take my resting heart rate." She put down the emery board, lay on the floor, and put her fingers to her throat.

"We're talking to the network about using the pilot as a midseason replacement. I'm going to put this statement up; picks me up to see it." He thumb-tacked the statement to his bulletin board. "We're holding out for six weeks. Be a lot of work for me."

"Maybe you should get away before all the work starts. I think you should go to that guy I went to on biofeedback."

"I tried to explain to Zoltan I don't feel right about the checks bouncing in Plonktown, but I couldn't make a dent. You talk to him and somehow you don't get--"

"I don't know why you get yourself in an uproar over those people. That kind of stress will kill you. I mean, nobody looks out for you, right? So why are you looking out for them?"

"Maybe it would be a good idea to go see this guy." He picked up a flyer from the mail.

"The biofeedback guy?"

"The real estate guy, the one keeps sending us lists. We could just see what he's got."

"Herb?" Stacy jumped up and massaged the back of his neck. "You know that new health club opened on Sepulveda? It's real nice; they have just everything, and I hear it's beautiful, everything brand new.

"Diesel took me."

"You rat, you went there and you didn't take me?"

"It was business. I told you, I went with Diesel."

"It's real convenient. They open at 6 A.M. and they even park your car. All my friends are going there. So could we join now?"

Boland tilted his head to the left, stretching the cords in his neck under her fingers, then reversed direction.

"Exercise really helps creative people," she urged. "Opens up your chakras."

"My what?"

"Your chakras, the energy centers in your body; there are seven of them, exercise helps so the ideas can flow."

She counted off the chakras for him from her forehead to her crotch.

"Sure." He shrugged his shoulders, then rolled them. "I wouldn't be so tired if I took time to work out, maybe take off a few pounds--"

"Great! I'll drive over and get us signed up today. I hope I can still get us in. You know, good places book up solid." She stopped massaging and threw her arms around his neck.

"Sure. We'll join. Why in hell not? Come in front of me, long lady. I got a chakra down here," he pointed, "needs attention immediately."

Chapter Eleven

"Listen, I want someone competent on that Rolls, and I mean right now. You guys have been farting around since Thanksgiving and this morning it stalled on me. On Sunset Blvd. In the morning rush!" Zoltan Diesel propped the phone on his shoulder next to the collar of his blue oxford cloth shirt, which was keyed in a darker blue than his tie; swiveled, and propped feet in bone colored sandals, no socks, on his glass desktop.

Diesel paused, listening on the phone. Avery Ford jumped up and waited, poised, at the corner of the glass desktop. Ford dressed carefully for this meeting, in a tan blazer, a crew neck brown cotton tee shirt, tan linen pleated pants, and white socks and Timberlands.

"I just got it back from you for its 20,000 mile checkup and it's not right. What did you do to it?" Diesel moved the phone from his shoulder and rotated his neck.

"Zoltan," Ford said, "we've got to talk. I know who cut down your trees. I can explain the whole thing." Ford wet his lips and began to pace the carpet between Diesel's desk and Herb Boland, who was leaning forward in the other chair, elbows on knees, his head on his hands, his eyes following Ford back and forth. Boland was wearing his standard going out outfit, black dungarees and a black tee shirt.

"Yes, I think you damaged something when you checked that Rolls. I do. It ran like a clock before I had it serviced at Thanksgiving. And your head mechanic's only suggestion so far has been to try to charge me again." Diesel slapped a bill from the Rolls Store next to the phone cradle. "So you get it fixed!"

"The clue that gave it away was that plastic hand they left you--" Ford carved the air with an index finger.

"Well, I don't know what's wrong, do I?" Diesel said on the phone. "That's why you're getting it back. Now, fix it." Diesel swiveled back and slammed the phone on the cradle.

"Zoltan, you're not the only one, let me tell you, there are more complaints about auto repairs to the consumer agencies than anything else," Boland moved his hands in a downward motion, calming.

Ford threw back his shoulders and drew in a breath, a declamatory moment. "It wasn't an accident; the crew didn't go to your place by mistake."

"All right, Avery, let's have it." Diesel put one hand on his desktop and tilted his chair back. "Are you drinking again?"

"No, I am not drinking--"

"There are, of course, residual mental effects after years of heavy boozing," Diesel arranged his tie, "without further drinking. You could be having those."

"See, the key is, they had to find out you were going to be away at that golf tournament that day. That took information gathering. They were organized."

"Believe me; I put a bee in that service manager's ear about what I thought of his service, and at these prices! That machine's going to be perfect when I get it back." Diesel said.

"Damn right." Boland nodded.

"Now, I'm running late today because of the damn car acting up this morning, so what is all this?"

"Zoltan, get unbusy, listen--"

"Herb, what is this crap today with Avery?" Diesel did not speak to Avery Ford.

"It's not my idea." Boland made a push away motion. "But Avery seems so convinced--" his voice drifted off.

"Somewhere along the line, Zoltan screwed the wrong person." Ford tried to step into Diesel's line of vision. "Like the Mafia, maybe. And they got revenge by wiping out his estate."

Boland and Diesel stared at Ford.

"It was the hand that tipped it off. You remember that scene in The Godfather with the horse's head in the guy's bed--"

"Jesus, I do not have time for this today." Diesel removed his feet from the desktop and swung his chair upright.

"All right, I'll prove it to you. Let me call that club where you were golfing that day." Ford ran around Diesel and retrieved the phone from the credenza, asked information for the golf club number, and dialed rapidly.

"This is Avery Ford, Mr. Diesel's assistant," he said. "He's left me with the job of sending out a press release on the golf tournament and I am in such a bind. I wondered if you had something written up, or if someone had already requested the information. Oh?" Ford's eyebrows made an arch. "You did? You wouldn't still have the number where you returned the call? Oh, that's great. I'm sure they'll have a release all written up." Ford grabbed the Rolls bill off the credenza and swiftly wrote a number on the back.

"The Mafia. They left a return phone number." Diesel said.

"That's just marvelous. I have to tell you, it's such a pleasure to deal with a person who's organized." Ford was on a roll. "You wouldn't believe the state of some people I have to talk to. Thanks so much."

"One more." Ford held up the hand with the receiver, avoiding Diesel's stab for it, dialing rapidly with the other hand. "It's an out of town number." He waited a few seconds. Then suddenly his face, which had been mobile with excitement, went blank.

"Well?"

"I don't understand it." Ford slowly replaced the phone. "It's a pay phone."

"Avery, for God's sake, I don't know why I even listen to you!" Boland stood up.

"Wait, what's this area code, could it be Plonktown?"

"It's a good thing you stopped with the booze. You're getting the d.t.'s."

"A minute," Ford said. "If it's Plonktown, that's got to mean something."

"Brilliant." Diesel rubbed his eyes.

"I'm getting an idea." Ford was pacing again. "See, this thing took research. Research — a library. I used to spend a lot of time in that library up at Humboldt State University while we were in Plonktown--"

"Really? Hardly where I'd have thought to find you, Avery." Diesel said.

"Since I got on the program. See, I never realized how much my life was organized around drinking. I don't see much of people who drink a lot now because it's boring sitting around sucking up Cokes while everybody else gets drunk. Beside, they get mad and tell me I'm no fun."

"They may have a point." Boland said.

"Anyway, let me tell you, there aren't a helluva lot of places you can go in Plonktown when you don't drink. So I spent a lot of time in the library, and there was this woman, a sort of big woman with red hair, the librarian. That woman had an attitude of getting things done."

"Is this what this is about?" Boland's head swiveled to follow Ford's pacing. "You have a letch for a librarian?"

"Is this discussion going anywhere?" Diesel asked. "I mean, does it have a point?"

"I think the librarian from H.S.U. in Plonktown knew where you were the day your trees got cut down! She found out by calling the golf club." Ford poked the air as he produced this information.

"How would she know to call the golf club?" Diesel looked at him.

"I don't know." Ford admitted. "But don't you see? If that's a Plonktown area code, that's got to have some connection with cutting your trees down!"

"Avery, I told you at the gym, your psychological fixation with these people in Plonktown is getting old really quick."

"Damn right," Boland said.

"It's not a fixation--"

Diesel leaned back, shut his eyes, and massaged the bridge of his nose. "Avery, you came here today because you thought I was under attack by the Mafia--"

"Okay, so that was wrong--"

"Now you have this new scenario you and Herb have devised--"

"Zoltan, I have absolutely nothing to do with this." Boland yelped. "I never heard a word about this librarian business until right this minute, so help me God."

"Avery," Diesel opened his eyes and raised his left index finger. "Herb has his work to do. We are supposedly getting together a package on a new western I just acquired."

"Well, sure, I know that--"

"I want the western to start shooting in February, before I deal with the Plonktown pilot, because I've got the financing lined up and I have to move on these things when the money is ready. Do you understand that so far?"

"Well sure, Zoltan," Ford said. "We're all set on casting me for the older cowboy."

"I've got some wonderful ideas on this one, very adult western, mythic overtones. I may do some of the writing myself."

"Uh," Boland started to bite a hangnail. "Zoltan, the western should be a coherent whole, one writer, I'll write it."

"Two," The middle finger went up. "I have found Herb gets distracted easily, and you are not helping with this crazy nonsense."

"I can't believe you guys don't see this--"

"I see it." Diesel said. "We're under attack by a librarian from Plonktown and she cut down all my trees."

"You certainly jump to conclusions, Avery." Boland crossed his knees and twisted one foot behind the other ankle. He started picking at the white lint on his black pants.

"I don't give a rat's ass how busy you two guys are, this thing is so obvious--"

"This idea is particularly ludicrous," Diesel tapped his ring finger, "because if you could remember all the way back to last month, you'd realize there wasn't a librarian involved in the film. No librarian. No motive to rise up and strike us all down, you see."

"Avery, maybe all that crap you drank burned out your brain." Boland said.

"In addition," Diesel raised his last finger, "such behavior is contrary to my considerable experience of how people behave under stress. When the matter is correctly set up, they don't have a focus during their brief period of being upset."

"But if it's Plonktown, what else could it mean--"

"And have you checked by calling up north to see if super librarian has been absent from her post?"

"I haven't had time; I just figured it out--"

"So, uh, you just came up with this idea?" Boland asked.

"And I am becoming uncomfortable having you in the western currently being packaged."

"What?" Ford stopped in mid stride.

"The western is an expensive package. I am responsible to the backers. I cannot justify having a lead who is delusional."

"But I'm perfect for the role. The casting director already decided--" Ford's face paled, showing for the first time a sprinkling of freckles along his cheekbones.

"Maybe I'm being a little too subtle for you, Avery, but I don't think you're behaving rationally, and frankly, that affects your work."

"Zoltan," Ford put his hands on the desk, palms down. They were sweating and they left prints. "You don't want me to discuss the trees any more, fine. I won't discuss them. Not a word."

"Good."

"I mean, all this about trees, I don't know anything about trees."

"That's right, you don't."

"This has nothing to do with the role I read for. These trees, I'm getting tired of all this about trees anyway. It doesn't lead anywhere, we'll drop it."

"Except," Diesel leaned back, "if I'm dependent on an actor who's not fully with us mentally, that is a risk to the production and I expect to pay accordingly."

"Now, Zoltan--" Boland began to untangle his legs.

"I'll call your agent, Avery. I'm sure he'll understand."

"What the hell does that mean?" Ford stood stiff.

"Equity minimum." Diesel said. He pressed a button the phone behind him. "Put my calls through now," he said to his secretary.

Ford's gray eyes flicked. He seemed to be waiting for some sign from Diesel, a recognition of who he was; a pause for argument.

Diesel waved a free hand as his phone call buttons started lighting up.

"That's all."

Chapter Twelve

About two hours north of San Francisco, Highway 101 changes shape. The redwoods start hunkering down on the highway, coming closer, backed by the hills, until above Garberville, where the highway alternates between dark tunnels of trees and clearings of sweeping vistas as the hills become higher and the highway cuts into their sides. The highway changes from a six-lane super highway to a two-lane blacktop with intermittent sections of a third passing lane. Gray-haired tourists in Winnebagos plug the highway in August; he and she sitting in front wearing cotton caps, unsure how to drive the curves, trailing 20-car lines of sweating locals. Sane people stay off Highway 101 as much as possible, August, or drive it at the crack of dawn.

Jenny Poway was driving south in a green Ford Country Squire with a bumper sticker that said 'All Mothers Are Working Women'. She was not going to cry. She was very determined about that.

The tourists hurry back to Riverside County or wherever, with the coming of the first torrential fall rains, which hit the streets of Plonktown so hard the drops bounce. Then the Mad and the Eel Rivers flood and carry whole uprooted trees to batter the bridges, and chunks of Highway 101 have been known to break off and fall in the rivers, and the residents wear yellow slickers like a Winslow Homer painting, because nothing else holds out that rain. Plonktown becomes isolated sometimes during fall storms, unable to get supplies from the south.

The locals know when the rains are coming because they watch the smoke from the two ugly old pulp mill smokestacks at the lip of the bay, visible all over town. The smoke fuming from the tall smokestacks makes a brown crayon line low on the horizon. Smoke blowing north means rain, because the storms sweep in off the Pacific; bounce off Cape Mendocino; and roar north up the Humboldt Coast. The only students who ride their bikes to Humboldt State University when the smoke is blowing north are the freshmen.

Local environmental groups attack the fumes from those mills every year. They never get anywhere. The mills provide a 20 million dollar a year payroll in an area starved for jobs.

Jenny knew she would be very composed, a Zen-like composure, just tell Herb about the baby and see what he said. At least she'd know what he had to say, if he had been serious about her. Because she had to know; she couldn't spend the rest of her life with her affair with him sort of not ended.

And she was going to tell Herb what Bart and Elwood and Tom and them were up to. She was going to warn him. Herb would appreciate that kind of candor in her.

God, how she missed him! She would go to sleep thinking about what he told her, and a day she didn't see him was no day. His sense of humor, his craziness, the stories he told her about people on TV, about what really went on at the sets, him talking, always talking, waving his hands, her listening and singing in his ear, a joke between them, 'You've made my life so glamorous, you can't blame me for feeling amorous.' And he told her there was a writer he liked, Dennis Potter, who understood the potency of old popular songs and put them in his plays to show a mix of feelings. And he would laugh and swing her off the sand at the beach. She felt cut off now, as if she had been reading a wonderful novel and didn't know how it ended.

How could she live her life without him? It wasn't just the baby. Bart would agree to raise the baby; he was a good man that way. They had tried for 8 years for one of their own. That's why she was so sure this one was Herb's.

It was his intensity. He nailed her ass to the bed. She had never known such intensity, such fierceness of desire. She watched other men now, speculating if they could be like Herb.

One time he took out clear fishing line.

"Open your legs," he said.

"What?"

He tied a knot to a clump of her pubic hair, deep between her legs.

"Bring that line up and let some hang outside your jeans," he put his mouth near her ear. "When there are people around, I want to pull it and you'll know I'm thinking about being inside you, high and hard. I want you to have to keep a straight face and talk normal to people while you get wet for me."

Was she supposed to give that up for Bart's boring 20 minutes a week of sex? She read somewhere that there was a survey and more than 50% of women said they'd choose chocolate rather than sex. She could believe it. These days she had trouble just lying still under Bart.

She had not consciously set out to get laid. She just wanted something in her life, to put on a pretty dress for once—which Bart hadn't even noticed—and go talk to a man. Bart was forever working. You'd think the world revolved around the damn gas station.

But events followed from putting on a pretty dress. Herb caught her when she was feeling good. It was one of Humboldt's warm summer days, no fog for once, and she'd spent the morning planning the new bathroom and talking to a couple of local carpenters, and she felt pretty.

She didn't fool herself. She had put herself in an occasion of sin. But she hadn't planned to get laid, just to flirt. And then, once it got started, the affair went on for weeks. She wondered if Sally and Marge, women she believed had active sex lives, ever felt this panic. Maybe they became hardened. Maybe they never had the panic to become hardened to. What was wrong with her?

The thing was that after Herb, her life seemed so boring, so reasonable and predictable, with no space for herself or for the questions she had started asking herself.

Back when she finished high school she thought about being an actress or even on TV. But the hand of reality was heavy on her shoulder; her father got laid off at the mill, and she had taken a job bussing tables, and then waitressing in one of the tourist fish restaurants in Eureka. Then Bart came along and her life seemed formed. She didn't see it as a waste. But being with Herb made her think different. He peeled back her eyes for her.

It was almost a 12 hour drive, even though she went 80 on parts of Highway 5 near Fresno, the cowshit run. A Northern California joke, this name for the straight run of highway, because just south of Fresno it was lined by vast fattening pens, with cattle so closely packed on a treeless plain that from a distance they looked like a moving brown cloth, and even in early December, like now, the pungent smell of manure steaming in the San Joaquin valley heat was strong enough to bring a tear to Jenny's eye. Northern Californians resisted driving south, and this introductory vision to the future intestinal tract of Los Angeles did not lure.

By the time she got to Southern California and then to Venice the small of her back and her neck both ached, and her eyes were burning and dry. For the occasion she had worn her best pink silk blouse, with a little bow at the neckline and long sleeves with 3 buttons at the wrists, and a loose navy blue skirt and jacket with brass buttons. She also wore stockings and low heels, which hurt her left toes because she hadn't worn anything but Birkenstocks or gum boots for so long.

It took Jenny 40 minutes to find a parking space and she finally settled for a one hour meter in front of a tacky looking drug store on Venice Blvd, a divided street with a bald median distinguished by sand glinting with broken glass and traffic signs saying No Left Turn. It was hot and she could feel the sweat between her breasts.

Venice surprised her. It was a shabby imitation of the picture in her mind. Herb said it was a crazy human mix, where adults roller skated for simple delight, and artists and musicians and crazies lived, and he made her laugh with his stories of haggling with the vendors in a sort of Persian bazaar along the Ocean Front Walk. But as she walked along Ocean Front Walk looking for his street the only vendors she saw were selling sunglasses and plastic cameras. And the people! Jenny saw a man; filthy, pants ripped down the back, and his behind hanging out.

She massaged the tension in her shoulders. Herb lived on a block that looked used, abused, and used again. It wasn't a street. The houses ran up both sides of a sidewalk from the ocean, and they were about 3 feet apart, and often even that space was filled with discarded furniture. The telephone poles held an incredible number of wires and some were tilted, with handwritten notices of garage sales and lost dogs stapled all over them.

What if the baby looked like Herb? Maybe if it moved like him, his shamble, his way of tilting his head.

She took a deep breath and rang the doorbell.

"Jenny!" He was wearing a pair of shorts and a tee shirt and she watched the surprise chase across his face before he smiled. "Great. Come on in, hon."

He didn't ask where she'd got his address, and she was glad. She'd called the studio and told them she had to forward a damage estimate for the gas station. It almost made her giggle, in spite of the way she was feeling. Some damage.

"My sweet northern lady; you smell of pine trees." He put his arm around her. "This is really a nice surprise; what are you doing in town? Let me get you a drink."

"No," she heard herself say, "I had to be in Los Angeles and thought I'd stop by."

"For sure." He nodded. "Uh, let me find you a place to sit in this mess." He cleared a batch of papers off an upholstered hassock and she sat.

Jenny's nose wrinkled at the smell of burning rope. No, wait. That wasn't burning rope. She was from Humboldt County; she knew what that smell was.

"Uh, look, Jen," he dragged in an office chair and sat opposite her, "I'm sorry for that business about the damn checks and the money, but you know that wasn't my fault. I really gave Zoltan hell about that, really went down to the mat with him."

"Well, Bart was pretty upset," she said. "But--"

"Of course," he nodded rapidly, "he feels promises were made--"

"Well, they were made, Herb. You made them."

"And you know I believed what I was saying." He said. "Hell, hon, some of the actors didn't even get paid. But it's not as if you're not going to get paid. The print of the pilot looks so good Zoltan's agreed to let me try some other ideas I came up with--"

"You're going to work again with Zoltan Diesel?"

"Jen, I explained to you, without money I can't operate. And there aren't many money men in the business."

"I can't believe you'd work with him again. He's a liar and a thief."

Herb looked upset. "You're not as patient as you used to be."

"You know what? I think I'm entitled not to be patient."

"Well, I do need to work with him. But I sure wouldn't let him hurt you or Burt."

"Bart."

"Bart, sure."

Jenny took another deep breath. This wasn't going the way she had planned.

"Uh, and I'm sorry I didn't get back to say goodbye, you know--"

"You didn't even phone."

"But things got so completely crazy there at the end, and--"

"Herb. It doesn't have to be the end."

"Jen, what is this?" His unkempt eyebrows made a chevron frown. "Some kind of test you're putting me through?"

"I'm not bitter about the money, you know that's not who I am."

Herb crossed his knees and jiggled one foot.

"I don't even rule out the possibility of marrying you. But we would have to be honest with one another."

"Yeah, honest." He looked at her.

"I'm honest with you, Herb. I came to warn you about something; there's something going on you have to know--"

"Jen, look," he swiveled farther away from her, "nothing's forever in this world. There's no way I'd go into another marriage. I mean, I've done it twice and it's just not for me."

"Well, I thought we could see each other." She swallowed saliva. "Once in a while."

His expression became smooth. "Jen, what we had together was really beautiful and I'll always treasure it. I can't see a pine tree without thinking of you."

"You need a tree to think of me?"

"But when it's over, it's over. We both have lives."

The speech came across well. As if he had used it before. As if he knew how to prey on women, just what to talk to them about and what their vulnerable places were.

"Because I think of you all the time." She twisted the strap of her purse around her index finger.

"Honey?" A young blond woman in green sweats and sneakers came through the screen door from the back yard. Jenny thought she had a Southern California look—she was about 10 years younger than Jenny. There were no horizontal rings on her tanned neck. Her shirt gaped above her pants, showing a tanned indented waist. Her hair was straight and blond and hung to the middle of her back. Jenny reached up and tentatively touched her own braided hair. The baby wasn't showing yet, but she had put on 15 pounds since her marriage and now there was a roll under her tits.

"Honey," the young woman said, "I can't get that charcoal to light and I've tried and tried."

"In a minute," Herb turned his head, "just talking to a friend."

A friend?

"I don't think you could be honest, Herb." She stood up. "You're very good at lying. You've been doing it a long time."

"Lying? I didn't lie to you, Jen, never." He said. "We always told each other it had to finish--"

"What a flabby character you are! You admit everything and make it sound like I chased you around. Sure, we'd say it had to end, but you used that to get me nostalgic, and we'd wind up in bed!"

"Jen, Jen, I didn't force you into bed. I thought you were glad."

She felt such intense pain she was afraid to speak, that her voice would crack. She understood the words coming from his mouth but they didn't seem to be Herb's words.

"I swear to God," he shook his head, "I do not understand why something so nice always has to end in bitterness. It's crazy."

For some dopey reason the words of the Peggy Lee song came bouncing into her head, 'Is That All There Is?' And she hated that kind of tackiness, couldn't believe it of herself.

The blond came through the back door. "Herb, if you don't start the coals, stuff isn't going to be ready," she whined. "I mean, these are your friends coming. I don't even eat meat."

Jenny knew she had to get out. She wouldn't be able to keep from crying for long. She started for the door, almost a run, turned an ankle with one of the damned heels, and crashed over the hassock.

The blond was standing in the doorway, gaping.

"Jen, wait a minute, honey," he picked her up and she knocked his hands off. He followed her down the front steps and into the concrete walkway. She was limping. He reached for her again.

"Leave me alone!"

"For Christ's sake, Jen, you hurt yourself! Would you stop for a minute?"

"Just let go of me."

"Jen, talk to me. What the hell is it with women that things have to end this way? And you said something about warning me, something was important--"

"No," she said, across her shoulder. "Fuck you."

Chapter Thirteen

"Stacy, hon, please stop yelling. I cannot believe this week with everybody yelling--"

"You have no goddam feelings, that's what's wrong. All you have is tunnel vision about the stupid TV shows you work on." Stacy Wade leaned a hip in seersucker shorts against the green lower kitchen cabinets to slam a cabinet door.

"Stacy, calm down. Radio Station C-A-L-M--"

"That woman, Jenny, was really screaming here yesterday and it upset me too, and I know something's going on with you and her."

"Stace, look, I am not promiscuous. It really upsets me when you say stuff like that." Herb said.

"It should upset you! I don't like this one way arrangement where I'm faithful and you're messing around. I mean, we agreed." Stacy stomped across the kitchen, tan legs beneath the shorts, above them wearing a tan tee shirt that showed a duck in a circle and said 'Venice Canals Waterfowl'.

"You get yourself all worked up over things that are really silly--"

"It's not that I don't have guys smelling around, you know." She started vigorously chopping lettuce into a wood bowl.

"You've got it all wrong with Jenny; she was just a friend up north. I mean, Stacy, come on."

"Some friend--"

"And she's gone back up north and I can guarantee you'll never see her again."

"That doesn't change what you did--"

"And I have good news for you and you're spoiling it." Herb put his arm around her waist.

"What good news?" her eyes slid sideways up at him.

"I don't know if I should tell you; you're being such a bad girl--"

"Oh come on, now, don't tease."

"Okay. Ta-dah!" He handed her a slip.

"My registration slip for Pico Tech! All right! You know how long I've been busting my ass to get in that ceramics course?"

"And Ta-dah!"

"What?" she made a grab for it.

"In today's mail, another statement from Nebula, with another bonus. Apparently it's some kind of regular thing they've set up."

"Herb!" she shrieked, and hugged him. "They're going to send you this much money every month? Wait'll I tell my friends--"

"Well, it's not that much of a surprise. I am worth it, after all. I know guys were gofers when I was already directing have been making this kind of money for years."

"Herb, we can do a lot of things--"

"Oh, so now I get a little more understanding."

"I'm still mad about that woman. You creative bastard."

"I'm a creative bastard and I've got a creative urge--"

"Herb, I told you, in the daytime people walking by can look in and see us on that porch--"

"So come over here on the couch." He propelled her. "That's all gone, of course. We're gonna get another place."

"Herb, a house! Can I help look?"

"I'll call that real estate guy today."

"We could get a fixer--"

"I'm sure as hell gonna need some tax shelter, so we better get a house right after the first of the year."

"Herb, honey, can I decorate it? We don't need a professional decorator; I've got lots of ideas and I've got piles and piles of pictures from Sunset magazine."

"This is supposed to be a good time of year to buy. The paper said the market drops dead around the Christmas holidays."

"I'd like to do something in a sort of high tech Craftsman. It would really go with the beach. Please, Herb, please?"

"Of course, I don't know how long Nebula is going to go on doing this. I just sort of assume it's going to continue."

"Well, give them a call--"

"No way. That's the wrong thing to do. Sounds like I don't expect it."

"If we get a wood house like this I'd take out the ceilings and go up to the roof for some skylights. Sunset is always doing that. They call it opening up the box."

"Listen," he was taking off his bathing suit, "let's get away for a couple weeks. I want to go out to the desert to a spa, soak up some rays, breathe some clean air, have a massage before I start the western. I may have a massage every day I'm there. God, I really ache."

"Oh Herb, I can't," she wailed. "I've absolutely got to start the ceramics course. They drop you if you miss the first class. And I need to take some decorating courses now, too. One of my friends said they have a woman teaching decorating who's really good."

"Tell you what, Hon," she pulled him down on her, "you go ahead. I'll take care of everything here. You," she started walking her fingers down his buttocks, "don't worry about a thing."

Chapter Fourteen

Wine was flowing at a holiday celebration at Tom Harly's house. Tom had put red and yellow ornaments on a small evergreen tree in a tub, a live tree. It was a live tree because he refused to have a cut Christmas tree in the house. He was like a kid about Christmas and he was glad he was giving a party, and he was wearing a long-sleeved forest green tee shirt and his Christmas suspenders, which had little Santas.

"—So then I found out the statue of Josiah had boxer shorts," Henry Richard said.

Brilliant weather. Most of December had been dripping wet, but today was clear and splendid; the afternoon filled with sun; long rays with dust motes shafting between the redwoods around Tom's house, the forest alive with stirrings, birdcalls, the creeping of insects. Under dripping ferns were secret gardens; the shoots of next spring's irises just broke the surface. There was a loamy smell to the forest as it gathered itself for winter. The doe and fawn who regularly nibbled Tom's roses had disappeared into the forest for the day.

"Henry, get to the red boxer shorts. Talk loud while I do the squid," Tom said. "Squid should be great. I drove up to Trinidad this morning to buy it fresh off the dock." Tom walked in the kitchen and lightly sautéed some garlic cloves in olive oil and dusted the cleaned squid with breadcrumbs. The oil made a soft spitting noise as the first squid hit it. He had put out a large wood platter of cut carrots, celery and cut cheese cubes, which was being decimated, mostly by Bart Poway.

"Well," Henry was wearing a shirt in deep cranberry with a bright red tie and black Sansabelt slacks, and he wriggled his behind, getting more comfortable in the chair. "I've been cleaning Josiah's statue in my studio."

Tom Harley walked back. "Josiah's statue's in your studio?"

Henry stopped. "Because of Sally."

Sally was sitting on the floor in a child's posture, knees in blue spandex in a zigzag, feet in cowboy boots. "I didn't like the film company, right from the start. And I didn't like moving Josiah's statue. So Henry said if I was that worried, we could put it on the work table in his studio. That way we could keep an eye on it."

"Right," Henry said.

"And it's a good thing we did," Sally said. "Because with the film company bugging out, we wouldn't even know where they stored Josiah. Can you imagine running around trying to find him?"

"Anyway," Henry recaptured the floor, "I've been cleaning Josiah's statue. It's been up there since the 30's and I figured this was a good opportunity."

"Yeah, and Henry made me haul Josiah from the plaza in my pickup," Elwood complained, "and I damn near got a double hernia when we lifted it up on the table at his place."

"The thing is, Elwood is so strong," Sally cooed. "They moved it, only him and Henry. They just balanced it beautifully."

"Well," said Elwood. "Well, being a logger, you have to learn to balance heavy stuff."

"Jesus Christ," Marge's voice was disgusted.

Sally shot her a look and unfolded off the floor without using her hands. Every male eye circled round. She poured a big glass of wine and brought it to Elwood. "Elwood, honey, you get a big glass of wine. That scam of yours went off so great."

"We all helped," said Henry.

"Well," said Elwood. "Well, thank you." His oblong face flushed.

"You can never get at that statue when it's up in the square," Henry raised his voice over Elwood's customary boom. "And I learned how to patina bronze when I was an art major in college. I started at the head. First I had to knock off about 2 pounds of pigeon shit."

"The red shorts--" Tom said.

"Well," Henry said, "you know the story about the statue."

"That it was originally cast in San Francisco during the Depression for some town up the road," Sally said, "but the truck broke down going up the hill and the truck driver got disgusted and just left Josiah's statue, and that's how come this place is called Plonktown, for Josiah Plonk."

"Would you let him get to the shorts--"

"Let him tell it his way." Sally said.

"And some of the college kids decided one year Josiah was politically incorrect, being a lumberman the way he was. Last year the thumb sported a white condom for a couple of months," Elwood said.

"And of course, there was the thumb-napping," Tom said.

"The what?" Sally asked.

"Oh, somebody broke off Josiah's right thumb and stole it, and left a stump where the thumb was. City Council put out a reward for its return, $500, but they never got it back. Had to have a new one cast by some guy in the Humboldt State University art department," Tom said. "Look at the thumb and you'll see. They couldn't get the patina to quite match because the statue had been out in the weather since the '30's."

Tom threw another handful of squid into the oil and watched as the rings began to curl and sizzle. A smell of cooked garlic filled the kitchen. The oil spit and Tom jumped back, sucking his thumb.

"So the statue was on its back. And you know how Josiah is wearing a sort of frock coat? Well, up underneath there it's painted bright red!"

"And we were really surprised." Sally said.

"And that's the flat bracing for his coat, goes from back to front. So it looks exactly like red boxer shorts. You could see them if you stood near the statue and looked up when it's standing in the square. I'm going to leave them that way."

"Gives a whole new side of Josiah's character." Tom said. "Maybe from when Plonktown was a red light district."

"Plonktown was a red light district?" Sally asked.

"Well, uh, the guys were up in the lumber and mining camps for months. And they came down to town when they got paid and needed supplies. And the idea was to relieve them of their pay as fast as possible." Tom said.

"Aw, the red paint has nothing to do with that," Elwood said. "I'll bet if you looked up the old police records down in the basement at City Hall, you'd find out some college kids painted Josiah during a football game."

"Right, and the city fathers got a lowball price on taking off the paint," Henry said, "so the guy didn't do the inside."

"The city got a cheapie job." Marge said.

"At least that hasn't changed," Tom said. "Ready now. You got to watch this squid and get it out fast." He scooped out the squid onto a paper napkin in a basket, squirted it with lemon, and passed it around.

"Umm, crunchy." Sally said. "I didn't know you could cook that good."

"Marge won't let me tell other women. She's afraid you'll gang up and kidnap me."

"Is that the same stuff you use for bait when you go fishing?" Bart Poway looked dubious.

"I'm making some other stuff." Tom used a long wooden spoon to stir white navy beans with carrots and a ham hock in a huge pot on top of the wood stove. He had used the black cast iron pot he called El Grande, 2 feet across, with a domed lid and heavy enough, empty, to be used as a weapon of defense.

"No complaining about the food at Elwood's victory party." Marge said.

"And you were right about it's being the most fun I ever had." Tom said. He grinned and refilled several wine glasses with exaggerated care and gestured a broad invitation, both hands holding the gallon bottle. He fell over sideways.

"Papa Cribari's best, grown in the purple shadows of the California hills, makes purple wine--"

"You're drunk." Marge was not a woman built to snuggle, but she snuggled now with Tom. "I can always tell. You start talking the purple hills of California, you're sloshed."

Tom looked at her triangular face in the light of the wood stove, high cheekbones, wide set eyes. She was smiling, showing teeth a little uneven. He liked them. Straight teeth made him nervous, ever since he'd had to pay for Yancey's braces. For the party she was wearing a black turtle neck and a floor length cotton skirt from India with horizontal bands of red, green and black, over black tights and Timberland walking shoes. He liked the skirt. She looked feminine. Made him horny, actually. Because most times she was dressed like she was playing on a soccer team.

"Working together, it was—I don't know, it was like playing, when you're a kid." Tom said. "I guess we lose that. When we do play now it's tennis or something, against each other. Not together, not teamwork."

"So when's my turn?" Marge asked.

She was ignored.

"I don't want to come," Sally prompted. "But if Marge wants to come on a scam, I think she should. I mean, the women are in this or we're not, right?"

"I don't see why we can't have some regular party food, this is a Christmas party." Bart complained. "Chips and things. I'm partial to that onion soup dip you have on chips."

"Although I near to dropped dead when that Avery Ford showed up." Elwood took a big gulp of wine.

"Strange guy, Ford." Tom said, making room for his plate on the floor. He speared himself several squid rings, which were fast disappearing from the paper napkin, and refilled a large glass of wine.

"You guys were lucky to get by Ford," Marge said. "I talked to him when he was up here; he used to be around the library. There's a lot going on under that perm. He's not as stupid as he looks."

"Not lucky," Elwood put down his glass, "we went for the odds. Goddam balls the size of grapefruit, we have."

"Well," Henry said, "I sort of--"

"All of us," Elwood said. "Goddam balls."

"Wait a minute," Marge said, wiping her mouth with a napkin. "I don't have balls and I helped and I think I did a pretty good job."

"You want honorary balls?" Tom lifted his head, which had been lolling on his chest.

"That's just the kind of male insensitivity we're talking about," Marge said. "That's the reason you guys ask us to help set up the scams and then won't take us with you."

"Elwood was using balls as- as a generic term," Tom soothed her.

"Well, there's got to be a female equivalent," Marge said, "and Elwood should use it."

"Jesus Christ, how come we always get back to this feminist crap?" Elwood said. "I can't open my mouth."

"Anyway, Herb Boland's neighbor in Venice says he's gone to a spa in the desert for the Christmas holidays," Marge said.

"Sounds like he's come into money." Tom smiled.

"How did Yancey change Boland's residual statements?" Sally's fluty voice rose above the roomful of conversation. "I know he knows about computers--"

"Beats me," Tom said. "He says he put in a virus. That's a set of planted instructions they don't know about, and it gets into their computer."

"You mean he did it from up here?"

"He's got time to sit around thinking this stuff up. I just got a letter telling me he got out of taking the calculus class at the high school. He aced the test."

"So then the way I get it," Bart made a frame with his hands, "he puts in an instruction that changes things once--"

"No." Tom shook his head. "The program can copy itself onto the company's master operating system, Yancey says, and that way the mistake happens whenever the software is used. Forever, or until they catch it."

"That's scary," Bart said.

"Exactly. Good thing Yancey's a good kid because I sure wouldn't know what in hell to do with him."

"Don't seem to me you have to worry; you were talking about your kid getting ripped off." Bart splayed his hands and examined his fingernails. "Seems to me he can take care of hisself. His own way."

"Well, he's mature about some stuff. He froze his credit card in a big ice cube in the freezer."

"Say what?"

"Froze it. The credit card I got him for when he goes to Sybil. Says that way he can't use it without thinking about it a couple hours while the ice is melting."

Bart looked at Tom.

"The thing to remember is, we can't relax now," Elwood said. "Because Bart's scam is really going to require timing."

"I got at that Rolls of his," Bart said, "setting there in his garage like a turkey on a table."

"Bart, if you'd just tell us exactly what you're doing, it would help." Henry said. "Instead of making everything a big mystery."

"Yeah, Bart," Marge said. "When you asked me to find out about the patrols near Diesel's house I thought you were going to steal his Rolls."

"No way. I don't want no Rolls. I want the money they owe me."

"So then I don't understand what you did to the Rolls."

"It'll start giving him trouble. Now we let him fiddle trying to get it fixed, a couple weeks."

"And then?"

"Then the rest of the scam. And Diesel put a repair on his credit card. I took one of the slips off the front seat."

"What good does that do us?" Henry said.

"Now we've got his Visa number," Marge said.

"I called a guy I used to work with," Bart said. "He's at a Rolls agency in Simi and he'll relay the call. I gave him a fake reference when he was hired, so he owes me."

"Okay, we know Diesel's schedule," Tom said. "And when he's likely to be driving the Rolls. I'll be ready with the tow truck."

"Don't you skin that tow truck, I'll kill you." Bart stood up. "I have to give you my new one. The old one has my name painted on it, with the Plonktown address so we can't use it."

"I've been practicing. I'm getting pretty good," Tom beamed.

"Yeah, well, cutting in and out of L.A. traffic with a tow truck is a lot harder than driving around Plonktown. And the timing is critical. You got to keep an eye on Diesel. Because if another tow truck gets to him first we've blown the whole thing. So keep practicing. One thing." Bart avoided looking at Tom.

"What?"

"The beard's got to go."

Tom put down his fork and his wine. "No way! It took me years to get this beard just the way I like it--"

"It looks wrong." Bart said. "I don't know no mechanics got beards like that."

"It just won't do, Harly," Henry said. "Now we agreed we'd do what was necessary; that's what we said when we started. And you don't look like a tow truck driver with that beard."

"Aw--"

"It'll make you look a lot different." Marge touched Tom's arm. "Just in case that kid from the telephone pole shows up again. 'Cause we'll be in the kid's neighborhood."

"Oh all right." Tom took a big gulp of wine.

"There's one thing, guys." Marge didn't bother looking up. "This time I come."

Tom met her eyes. "Oh God, not that," he groaned. "Tell me you're not going to make a stand now on going with us and screw everything up. Say it. Say you're not going to do that." But he knew she was not going to be cajoled or deflected this time.

"I thought we had this worked out," she said. "I thought we agreed I'd stay here for the first scam because you'd use the time to talk to the guys about me coming. But you didn't talk to them, did you. I mean at all?"

"Oh, no." Bart's big hand scooped up a bunch of American cheese cubes. "No way. We'd have to take care of you; it'd be more complicated. There's no way I'm taking a woman along when my scam goes down!"

"Would you at least listen--"

"No. Now that's the end of it."

Chapter Fifteen

Marge Fairweather was in 3rd grade when she found out she was better at schoolwork than the other kids, and the other kids hated her for it.

The occasion of her discovery was the school play, which the sisters did every year at Christmas. Marge's mother had firm ideas about education and devoted a big portion of her meager salary to paying the tuition at St. Ambrose Catholic School on what was then called Dago Hill in St. Louis, Missouri. Marge was the only non-Italian in her class. The class was roughly 70% Northern Italian and 30% Sicilian.

When the church was built in the 1920's, there was neighborhood uproar because St. Ambrose was a Northern Italian saint, being the bishop of Milan. The Sicilians, who arrived 20 years after the Northern Italians, mostly to work in a brickyard at the foot of the hill, threatened to build their own church. The bishop, who was Irish-American and therefore not familiar with the tower principle of Italian prejudice—every Italian looks down on everybody south of him—had to exercise his pastoral authority and demand the two groups in the congregation settle their differences. He heard the remarks of the Northern Italians, of course, about Southern Italians. "Meridionale," with a sneer. Or, "They all have knives in their pockets." The bishop rose above the fray.

The saint matter was settled by the establishment of a large side chapel next to the main altar, dedicated to Santa Rosalia, a Sicilian saint. This arrangement was in violation of canon rules about what could be adjacent to the front altar, but nobody was arguing.

It was against the background of this schism that the sister in charge of the annual Christmas pageant wrote in a role for Santa Rosalia. She cast Marge in the role, undoubtedly because Marge, as a non-Italian, freed her of accusations of favoritism. This sister was also Irish-American and kept rewriting the role and changing the lines as she was corrected by pointed comments from the parishioners.

The other kids couldn't handle the frequent script revisions; couldn't keep the lines straight. Marge would prompt them and the harassed sister would say, "Oh, just let her say it." By the time of the pageant Marge had most of the lines, but she had to get off the hill by a circuitous route to avoid being ambushed.

This incident shaped Marge. She was taller than the other children and could outrun them, which trained her to rely on her body to get her out of trouble. She also became a loner, filling her arms through elementary school with books about girls who solved mysteries and raised horses. At a time when all the other girls in class wanted to be ballerinas, Marge wanted to be a jockey.

She was inoculated by group exclusion against the subtle message to the girls on Dago Hill, that boys won't like you if you're too smart. In 8th grade the class took a diocesan achievement test, and the sister told Marge's mother they couldn't measure her reading level because it went over the top of the test. At the St. Ambrose 8th grade graduation the students lined up according to height to go on stage to receive their diplomas. Marge was last. Reluctantly, she cancelled her dream of being a jockey.

The Catholic girls' high school next year served the whole city, including a wealthy area surrounding Freedom Park. The school divided students into three tracks: academic, general, and business. Marge was the only girl from St. Ambrose to select academic, and she was surprised to be told by a counselor that her family was poor and she should take the business track and secretarial courses.

It had never occurred to her that her family of 2 was poor. Her mother worked 2 jobs, but they seemed to have everything they needed, and it was hard to think of themselves as poor when their back yard was a view of the sweep of the Mississippi. Marge took a closer look at the other students in the academic course.

All the students wore the plaid jumpers then in favor with Catholic schools, so you couldn't tell status from clothes. But some of the students wore their hair very different from Marge's, and seemed to speak, gesture, and even stand still in different fashion. The Freedom Park girls had their tuition paid in one yearly check and received things like horses for birthdays.

Marge took both academic and secretarial courses, which really upset the counselor. In her junior year she started working summers for an Office Temporaries agency. To her surprise, she liked the Office Temporaries work. The agency had plenty of work and since she was only at each office a week or two, she avoided the resident office politics.

She saw little of the girls from St. Ambrose. Several of them had dropped out of school. And she never really knew the girls from Freedom Park. So she spent her sparse free time at the library.

The library in the area was an old building and featured oak window seats in front of lead paned windows. Marge developed an affection for window seats; lead paned windows; and libraries. She read a lot of love stories about girls who weren't pretty.

College didn't seem an option. But then Marge got a state scholarship, which meant she could go to the State University at Columbia, provided she worked.

In Marge's junior year at Missouri State University the library science students were targeted by a feminist group that handed out tracts decrying female stereotyping in career selection, which included librarians. Marge's mother was ill by then with the cancer which was to kill her within a year, and Marge was taking all the office temporary work she could get. A student named Robin singled Marge out at a coffee hour at the Student Union.

"You get good grades. I assume you have a mind buried someplace under that wild hair," Robin touched her own streaked silken bob, "and you're binding your mind, like Chinese women bound their feet, except it's worse to do that to a mind. Our group needs help and we're in a real fight. You could help us by giving out literature on the quad. I see you haven't signed up for any hours on our schedule."

117

"I'm working," Marge set her coffee cup on the wide upholstered arm of a battered couch.

"At what?"

"Secretarial work." Marge selected two large cookies.

"Calories!" Robin's lips compressed. "How can you restrict yourself to low pay in female ghetto work?"

"See, I don't have a daddy to send a check; I have to work at something--"

"That means being someone's secretary? A secretary is a high class servant in business clothes. Doesn't your mind wander? I honestly don't understand how you focus on what you're doing."

"What's that?" Marge asked.

"What?" Robin stopped in mid argument.

"There." Marge pointed. "On your tit."

Robin looked down. "It's my boyfriend's Alpha Phi Alpha pin."

"Oh." Marge said. "Like branding a cow?"

She was not invited to a coffee again.

"Why don't you ever see any of the girls from St. Ambrose any more?" her mother asked one day.

"I ran into Lisa Salerno in Famous Barr the other day. Remember her? She was on the girls' basketball team with me. She was a pretty good forward. She's in that picture of the team in the school yearbook. She's pregnant with her second." Marge made a hospital corner on the sheet at the foot of her mother's bed.

"I remember her." Marge's mother tried to sit up. Marge braced her. Her mother wore a wrist watch but the watch flopped around to the wrong side of her skinny wrist. Marge helped her turn it back.

"She's living downstairs from her mother. She says it's great. Her mother helps with the 2-year-old and when she has the baby. When they were first married she thought they were going to have to live with her husband, Vinnie's, mother and she says that would make her crazy."

"That's wonderful." Her mother sighed. "Her mother will really get to know the grandchildren. It will be like one big family, like when I was a girl."

118

"In another few years her oldest will start St. Ambrose. The whole thing starts all over again."

"You think that's a bad life?" Her mother tried to find a comfortable position. "Maybe I made a mistake, pushing you so much with school."

"Different strokes for different folks, Mommy." She took her mother's thin hand.

On graduation Marge accepted an appointment at the research library at Humboldt State University. Her mother was dead and there was no longer anything to hold her in St. Louis. In Humboldt she rode her bike; she camped; she had an ease in her movements and her low-pitched, assured voice surprised people who had stereotypes of librarians.

Marge established a special collection of books on Alternative Energy; some of them privately published in paper wrappers, stored on a separate bookshelf. This collection proved inordinately popular, because the way you got caught growing marijuana indoors in Humboldt County was by high utility bills for your grow lights. People in Humboldt became experts on Alternative Energy; they built windmills; they built waterwheels, they burned cowshit to generate energy. Such a man, the minute he had a chance, would pointedly drop the line, 'I'm off the grid," meaning he was not connected to any power utility.

Timing is all. In the winter of 2000 out of state vendors cut back the electricity coming to California. Computers went down in midday; traffic signals malfunctioned; bills tripled and quadrupled. Suddenly everybody was desperate to learn about Alternative Energy.

Marge had the collection.

She loved the look of the Pacific Northwest as soon as she saw it, and decided to cement the relationship by buying herself a small hillside house, with a living room where she could watch the wild storms sweep in across Humboldt Bay. The front door of the house was shaped like a gumdrop and it was made of thick dark paneled wood with brass hinges and a huge brass latch and a brass kick plate across the bottom. Marge pictured herself as an old woman, still going through her door into her house.

119

When she told the only savings and loan in Plonktown that she was unmarried, the loan officer laughed heartily, called her 'little lady' and refused her loan. Marge paid a female attorney in Eureka $50 to write a letter discussing terms of qualifying and hinting at a possible discrimination suit. Marge received a call from the loan officer, sounding harassed, saying their loan committee had reconsidered, based on the fact that the university said she was on a tenure track, and congratulating her on the fact that they stood ready to make the loan.

Several of the men Marge was seeing at the time volunteered comments about her purchase of her house. She didn't have a termite inspection, and they told her she was crazy. There was a wet spot under the bathtub and they warned that could be a serious and expensive plumbing problem and could invite termites. The doors were wearing holes at the hinges, and they told her that could let termites get in the wood.

"There are other ways to look at house buying beside termites," Marge said.

"Tell me that when you fall through the floor."

Marge dropped the subject and bought the house.

But the first time she dated Tom Harly, he stopped dead in her living room and then walked over and stared out the wall of windows at the view of Humboldt Bay, the Mad river, the mountains, and two small towns.

"God, this place is really beautiful," he said.

Marge smiled.

"So let me get this straight; I did all the research on Boland and Diesel, and now Bart doesn't want me to come, and you agree." Marge, clad in green striped shorts over long sweatpants and New Balance shoes, finished her run with a sprint for the last quarter mile, muscular legs like pistons.

"My legs are tired. I'm going to feel this tomorrow." Tom Harly evaded her as he limped off the track. He sprawled on a park bench backward, his legs coming out between the seat and the back, his elbows braced on the top rung, his shoulders slumped, knees flopped open.

The Redwood Bowl at Humboldt State University was a quarter mile oval track with wooden stadium seats on the two long sides and a squat concrete gym on one of the oval ends. The other end was the redwood forest, giving the Bowl the impression of a natural cup on top of a mountain. The composition track occupied the highest spot on campus, up two acute hills. Runners could arrive puffing before starting their runs.

"Macho man, you tried to run faster than me."

"I didn't try, I did run faster."

"Only because you have longer legs. Get up. And stick to the subject, which is taking me south as part of Bart's scam."

"You were part of the scams; you got the information--"

"I supply the information on which men get things done?" she slapped a towel around her neck.

"Marge, I don't know how these scams are going to go down. Elwood's went off great, but we can't expect our luck to hold. Someone may catch us." Tom jumped as she threw the towel at him.

"And you think Henry's going to be more help in a crunch than I am?"

They headed for the exit near the gym and walked up a concrete ramp. The air in the early morning was fresh under the coastal fog; the students gone until the new semester started in late January, the track a vibrant terracotta around the green grass oval.

Tom Harly was unbowed. "I can't live with this. I have real anxieties about you coming with us. I'll be worried about you and I won't be able to do what I have to."

"Anybody ask you to protect me? I thought promised not to be like that. "

"Marge, if 3 or 4 guys can't get together and agree; can you imagine complicating it with a woman?"

"Oh." She stopped walking. "That's different. That's not about me, then. That's about the other guys might not want a woman."

"I know Bart doesn't want it and it's his scam."

"Then how come Sally's cooing over Elwood?"

121

"Sally's different."

"Why? Because she looks like a bimbo?"

"No, goddamit! Because she's more experienced with- with the world. And she doesn't look like a bimbo; she takes care of herself. She puts on makeup. It's all I can do to get you to have your hair cut."

"You want a woman with lipstick thick as peanut butter?"

"You're getting catty--"

"No, that's a description, not a judgment."

"And no, I don't like women with a lot of makeup. Why do I always wind up sounding like a total sexist when I talk to you?"

She grinned.

"It's not true--"

"And what about Jen, then?"

"Ah, there you have me. Frankly, I don't like Jen and I never have. She whines nonstop. So it's good that she doesn't want to come and she has zilch interest in what we're doing, even in what Bart's doing."

"Here's Bart, and he thinks because I'm a librarian I'm a wimp." She said. 'He's got that image—librarian goes with someone who dusts books and says 'shush'.

"Don't take it out on me if you don't like being a librarian--"

"I love being a librarian. It's the image you guys have of librarian."

They walked down the two steep hills, Tom walking gingerly, and turned into the community forest, following the tarmac that wound past houses at the edge of the college and then through ferns and fennel in dark shade, past a children's camp. A brook dripped, the ferns dripped, the tarmac glistened slick with dew, and where there was a clearing, knee-high grass waved in the now warming morning air.

"Look at that." Tom said. "See, that redwood was cut 20 feet up in the last century and a new redwood grew from the stump and now the second redwood is about 80 feet high above the stump, so you get nesting trunks. God, I love it here." He took a deep smell.

"Forest primeval," she said. "That's why old Josiah Plonk built his mansion right next to the lumber yard. He knew from trees. Wanted to keep an eye on his logs."

"I don't understand why you even want to come south with us! All those goddam people living on top of one another, and you breathe in what they breathe out—entire city smells like a fart."

"Oh, here we go, typical Humboldt native, got to look down on Southern California."

"I just don't like Los Angeles." Tom glared.

"Call it Iowa by the sea, and talk about smoggy days and Uzi-filled nights. You guys should be grateful for Southern California."

"For what?"

"Because if all those people weren't penned in down there, some of them would be up here."

"No they wouldn't, because those jerks couldn't take the weather. Which is why we're gonna sell them water when we become a separate state. I think that state senator who wants us to secede from California and be another state is dead right."

"Yeah, and did you see how that guy made the dividing line? It was supposed to be a simple line across the state under San Francisco, from the Pacific to Nevada. But he put in 2 bumps, to leave San Francisco and Sacramento as part of the south. Because people up here want to turn their backs on the cities and their problems. So San Francisco would be the northernmost city of Southern California. It's almost worth doing just for that."

"The cities have 90% of the population and we've got 7%. Which means their legislature tells us what to do."

"And what are you going to call this new state?"

"That's the least of our problems--"

"How about Baja Oregon?"

He stopped and looked at her.

"Did you know it said in the paper there was a movement up here before World War II," she continued, "Several counties in Northern California and Southern Oregon were fed up with paying taxes and getting no road building funds and they wanted to secede and form a new state together. They were going to call the new state Jefferson. They were all set to go; then the movement stalled when war broke out, but the attitude remains. So there's a precedent; you could call the new state Jefferson."

"You're killing me today."

"I'm on you because I'm hearing you think Bart's attitude is OK."

"This is Bart's scam and he has enough problems with organizing it, and with Jenny right now, without me insisting you come south with us."

"Don't you see, you're more worried about what Elwood and Bart think than about what I think? You're worried about Sybil thinking you're a wimp; what about what I think of whose side you're taking?"

"With all the details on the scams we've got to work out--"

"It has to do with hearing me. Seeing me."   Marge picked a dandelion out of the ferns and twirled it.

"I don't want to compete all the time. Not with my woman." He didn't look up.

"Fine, as long as you don't avoid competing by just assuming that male projects take precedence, because, see, that pisses me off." Marge blew the dandelion.

"Why can't you be supportive just once? Back me up, the way Sally backs up Henry."

"Nope," she looked at him. "Maybe we're going to have a problem with this. Not backing you. Beside you. Like Shaw says, a woman should be a consort battleship."

"Just what do you think you're going to do if you come South with us? I don't see much."

Marge threw away the dandelion and brushed her fingers. "What I'm seeing is that we're two very different people. I'm a systematic organized person. I plan things the best I can and then go for it. You get in the middle of something and wing it."

"Not true. Right now I'm practicing with the tow truck for Bart's scam--"

"That's why you couldn't plan your scam. You were lucky Yancey thought up that stuff about Boland's residuals."

"Oh, just because in the kitchen I told you I was upset because I didn't come up with a plan, now you bring it back and murder me."

"No, because it's true."

"You know, the people who matter to me—you and Sybil, and even Yancey—sometimes I can't talk to you. Because later you guys remember it and mug me. Makes me feel I have to go through everything important in my life mute."

The tarmac curved out of the forest to the street. They crossed the bridge over Highway 101 in angry silence, traffic humming through the bridge up through their heels. They turned left and walked to Tom's house.

"And I do know what I'll do in L.A." she said. "Diesel is going to get married."

"What?"

"Yeah, married. When we're down south I'll say I'm his assistant and order what he needs." She propped her elbows on the kitchen counter and looked at his wall calendar. "I think we'll name January 26th the big day, that's a Sunday. We'll tell them deliveries have to be that day or they can't have the order."

"What deliveries?"

"Diesel's going to need a lot of stuff: food, flowers—trees, of course. The wedding is going to be at his house. Oh, and new grass. He'll need lots of yards of turf. What are you cooking for breakfast?"

"An omelet with potatoes and eggs."

"You want me to cut the potatoes?"

"No, you get in the way."

"That's because you take up the whole cutting board."

"The cutting board is a turf war now?"

"It's the territorial aggression of the male."

"I don't even know if you're kidding," he looked at her. "That's how bad things are with us."

"Diesel's going to need chairs and tables. And of course wedding caterers, and the band. Baking powder?" she asked as he put some in.

"To make the omelet light."

"Would you stop sulking?"

"This is not sulking; this is thinking. Sometimes I sabotage myself. You know, I kill things in a relationship with someone I really like by going off on tangents." He paused in cooking. "I can never seem to just go along."

"This is the way it is. You going to help me with my scam down south or not? This is not a time you can perch."

He put the box of baking powder on the shelf and turned back to her. "You're serious about this."

"You have no idea."

"Okay, then, you come south."

"Good." She put her hand on his. "And Diesel will need a lot of press. I'll get a list of the news services. He's pretty well known. Don't let me forget the limos. They can bring them in on a flatbed. I'll use his credit card to guarantee it. But I'll just use the number for confirmation. I've got a better idea."

"What?"

"C.O.D."

Chapter Sixteen

"No. Now I said no, and that's that." Bart shoved his chair back from the coffee table.

"It's simple, Bart." Henry said. "We're going to have to cover Diesel from, say, 7 A.M. to midnight. If he takes out the Rolls when we're not watching, we blow it."

"That's not you guys' problem; you guys' problem is you're pussy-whipped--"

"OK, so that's 17 hours a day." Tom Harly said. "We can't let Diesel see you if you're going to get at the Rolls and I need to drive the truck so we can't let him see me. That leaves Henry and Elwood—it's too many hours. We need Marge."

"I already told you, there's no way I'm gonna take Marge. This is complicated enough--"

"We all make changes, Bart." Tom said.

Bart sighed morosely and looked around his living room. A full laundry basket was on one chair; piles of computerized monthly statements from the gas station spilled off another. "Look, I'm sorry I don't have coffee; something, not even a beer."

"We just came over for a few minutes." Elwood said.

Tom was glad Sally made Henry and Elwood come with him to speak to Bart. A united front.

"And I'm sorry about the house," Bart said. "The way it looks. Smells damp, since Jen decided on staying with her sister in Fortuna."

"It's fine--"

"Maybe Jen used to open the doors or something. Me, if I don't see the dirt, it don't bother me. So I just don't look. Here, I'll open a door." Bart struggled with an aluminum sliding door. It took two hands to push it a couple of inches.

"Bart, for God's sake, don't worry about it," Henry said.

"Maybe it's the bathroom." Bart paused. "It doesn't have the right kind of vent or something, and there are these black mildew spots that grow on the ceiling above the tub."

"Will you stop about the house? You didn't invite us, remember? We just called and said we had to talk," Tom said.

"I don't understand it. Jen worked like a beaver and never got anything done. I used tell her: if you open a jar, it's easier to put it right in the garbage instead of parking it in the sink or on the frig, because then you have to spend an hour picking up all the jars and cans." Bart looked around him. "I haven't been able to get somebody to clean."

"Bart, look, we just came to tell you what we decided," Tom said. Bart was right. He had to pee, but he didn't want to use the bathroom in this house.

"The house used to smell like food, because Jen used to keep my food warm until I got home at night, which was whenever, depended what was happening at the station. That's right, now I think of it. She used to."

"Look, Bart, Marge did a lot of work looking up stuff and now she wants to come," Tom said, "so what we wanted to say--"

"I didn't think much about it. The house; I just took things as they came. I figured, I was always working, since I was 14. Two jobs when I first started the station." He looked around, as if surprised to see his own house.

The tract house Bart owned had been built in the Bottoms by a Southern California contractor who operated in Plonktown briefly, until he discovered the houses he was building weren't selling. With their sliding doors and no wood stove, buyers turned them down because they were totally unsuited for the weather. Bart and Jen had bought the house cheap, but the sliding aluminum doors were on the West wall: they got the full rain from ocean storms and warped off their tracks; the roof had a low pitch, so the rain puddled; and the wood siding was splitting vertically because the eaves weren't deep enough to deflect the rain.

"I don't understand why, now it's my scam, you guys are making this big fuss about Marge coming." Bart moved the computer statements and dropped in the chair.

"Bart, I'm sorry you broke up with Jen," Henry said, "but you can't just not deal with women."

"I have trouble getting used to being here alone. It's been 8 years, married."

"Give yourself time--"

"She does my bills, you know, at the station. So no bills went out this month and I didn't get any money in. And I got the first of the year bills still to do, beside the first of the month. And I got to leave everything next week and go south with you guys."

"Well, what does Jen say?"

"Huh. There used to be an old hillbilly love song had a line, 'Once we tore down the wall and put in a door; now we don't speak anymore.' Yeah, that's it. Jen don't speak any more. Not about anything important."

"Why don't you go out some?" Elwood said. "Hunkering in here like a bear; it's no good for a man to sit around every night. Now, there are lots of pretty ladies at the Jumbo, down to Eureka. And music--"

"One of my gas jockeys; he says he can get $20,000 from his family. He wants to buy part of the station. I been thinking to give him a sneeze of the business. Then I could get away some."

They started to leave, following Bart through the sliding door, turning sidewise to get through, and even then Elwood had trouble. The yard was an oozing bog.

Bart leaned against an outer wall. "I been in harness so long, I keep going. I keep running the gas station. I keep smiling at the customers; keep their trucks running; fix their brakes."

"Bart, for God's sake, pull yourself together," Henry said.

"It's not acceptable, right? I mean, it's not acceptable that I hurt. I'm supposed to roll on to the next woman. Because that's what men do."

"You have to go on living," Henry said.

"I look the same, but it's as if I'm waiting inside. Everything's waiting."

"Maybe," Elwood said, "we better put off this thing with the Rolls--"

"No." Bart said. "It's important I do my scam. I tell you, this planning the Rolls thing; it felt good. It's important not to feel like a victim."

"Wait. Marge said that. Didn't Marge say that?" Tom Harly asked.

"I mean, it's Sunday, right? Jen used to cook something special Sunday, maybe roast a chicken. And I'm just sitting here, looking at these bills."

"Bart, see, we came to a decision." Tom said.

"I thought you guys were here to talk to me, make me feel better."

"We're not coming unless you let Marge come. With us." Tom said.

Bart looked at Elwood. "You part of this?" he asked.

"I think they're right."

"I notice nobody asked Elwood to take her."

"She's not going to cut down trees." Elwood said.

"So what do you think this is gonna be, an all-day picnic?" Bart stood in the rain, hair soaked now across his brow.

The others got in Elwood's truck and Bart walked to the door of the truck.

"Maybe the whole way I been doing things is wrong. What have I got? I haven't got a wife. Pretty soon I may not have a station. And so help me God, I don't understand it, because for years I been doing nothing but busting my ass."

"Bart," Tom said, "go inside. You're getting soaked, you're gonna get sick. The scam will work better if we take Marge."

"Oh for Christ's sake," Bart said, "take her!"

Chapter Seventeen

Herb Boland switched his canvas carryall to his left hand and pulled out his keys with his right as he swung around the corner of his walk street in Venice. He'd had to pull his car up illegally on the alley that served the walk street. It would be all right. Like most beach residents, Herb knew to the nanosecond the time he could risk to zip in, park illegally, and run inside on an errand. A wooden sign posted on one driveway on Herb's alley said "Fastest Tow in Town."

"—So today's the day everybody comes back from the holidays and we'll decide when they're going to do the western and whether I'm going to do it for them."

"The network has already agreed to the western," Avery Ford put his hand on Herb's arm. "That's why I wanted to meet right away. Now we need to get behind the Plonktown pilot."

"ABC is talking six shows of the western as a replacement in their spring schedule; Diesel wants thirteen. And you heard what they did to me."

"Have a peppermint," Ford snapped open a tube of Lifesavers with his thumb. "The thing is, maybe we should take what they've agreed to--"

"What peppermint?" Herb waved them away with his free hand, "They brought in an executive director to work with me if the Plonktown pilot flies. I've already got that asshole, Jax Davis, I have to explain everything to, including how to find his ass with both hands."

"Herb," Ford modulated his voice, an actor's trick, "is it the person or the fact that they're bringing someone in?"

"It's the nerve of their doing it--"

"Because, remember what we're doing here, we want this Plonktown series to air. We all got this far, we don't want to blow it. You remember the writers' strike, in '88, that was twenty two weeks nobody worked. That's what you get for stubborn in this town."

"The guy is okay—not the person I'd have chosen, mind. Watch out, Venice Easter eggs."

"What?"

"Dog turds." Boland pointed down at the sidewalk between the facing rows of houses. There were indeed several dog turds.

"So, Herb, you'll work with him--"

"It's just the idea of their doing this, after I brought in this concept of using a northern town, over everybody's objections. I saw Plonktown two years ago and I knew I was going to use it somehow. They fought me goddam tooth and nail and now, after the pilot's turned out great and when the network wants it, and they want a few changes, now they bring in somebody as executive producer. I may quit."

"Herb," Ford stopped walking. "I'm getting gray. I was having a haircut this morning and I realized my hair style was as old as my stylist. I think he thinks the way I cut my hair is less a hair style than an expression of nostalgia."

"What? Avery, what does your hair have to do with anything?"

"Because I've started looking at magazine ads now, Herb, to see how the models are wearing the gray. I'm getting older. I need people to see the Plonktown pilot."

"What do you want from me?"

"Somebody has to stay with the project, Herb. Somebody has to push. I keep going up to see Diesel. He won't pick up a phone until he finishes planting his damn trees. The studio must have said something to you, a reason for bringing in somebody else--"

"Jax Davis at the studio says he hears I'm drinking again."

"Oh."

"Which has nothing to do with this series. Don't start your reformed drunk act, Avery. Diesel is trying to get the Plonktown pilot to air in February. Now this new jerk wants changes. This is my series and I'm not going to let them castrate it. What in the hell?"

They had reached Boland's house. Boland stopped at his gate and stared, open mouthed, at the newspapers, magazines, and catalogs which cascaded down the six tilting wooden steps leading to his apartment. Mail was stuffed into the mailbox nailed to the wall next to his door and falling out on the covered porch.

Boland put down the carryall and picked up a handful of the mail. Each of the top letters was stamped in red URGENT. He opened a letter from a restaurant.

"What?" Ford moved from foot to foot.

"Some kind of screw-up." Boland shrugged. "Says my check has been returned by my bank and unless I make it good immediately they're going to proceed with legal action. A screw-up. Not what I need." Boland put the letter in his pocket.

He opened the front door, which required kicking a number of catalogs out of the way, and walked in the living room and called in a loud voice, "Stacy?"

The room was empty. No, it wasn't empty. There were four cardboard packing boxes. All of Stacy's paintings and books were gone, as were her rocker and the TV set. She had left the oak footstool.

"Oh, Jesus," he said to Ford, "she's walked out. And she cleaned out my bank account, because my checks are bouncing."

"Can she do that?"

"Two of my ex-wives did. It seems to be a thing women do. Of all people to have this happen to again, you'd think after twice I'd learn--"

"But you and Stacy aren't married."

"That's right." Boland paused, surprised. "You're right. Stacy wasn't on the checking account."

He walked into the sleeping porch. The mirrored door of the armoire they used as a closet hung open and Stacy had removed her clothes. Most of his were on the floor.

The note was taped to the rocks that formed the front of the fireplace with two foot long pieces of masking tape, crossed in an X with the note at the intersection.

Stacy said she had been at the health club with her friends when the manager had approached her and told her she would have to leave because of something wrong about his check and she had never been so humiliated and she had had it with him he was flaky and all week people had been

133

calling about bounced checks and screaming at her and she got so nervous she ate wrong and put on 5 pounds and she had dropped his whole mug of paper clips in the slot of his computer and she hoped he electrocuted himself.

The note was bereft of punctuation.

"There's some kind of confusion going on," he said to Ford. "I'll call the bank." He picked up the phone. It was dead. He looked at the pile of letters. There was one from General Telephone, also marked URGENT.

"Wait, they've cut off the phone. We'll call from the booth on Ocean Front Walk and tell them to put back service."

"No. First you call and find out what's going on with the pilot."

"Avery, you really get on something."

"It's how I live, Herb, I push."

"Okay, Okay, I'll call my agent, Nat."

"See, I had a pretty scary period, Herb. A dead time. I lost a decade while I was a drunk. So now I can't afford to lose any more time."

"A couple weeks I went on vacation and I was relaxed and I'm back less than an hour and my stomach is bothering me."

They walked down to Ocean Front Walk and Boland punched in a series of numbers at a pay phone.

"Does that phone work? It looks funny."

"It's fixed so you can make calls out, no calls in, so drug dealers can't use it as a phone drop."

"Oh." Ford said. He looked around. This part of Ocean Front Walk was a discordant combination of commercial lots occupied by tee shirt vendors under plastic awnings, side by side with single family residences with the kind of eye-popping architecture featured in **Architectural Digest** and **Abitare**.

One beachfront house had a single room in front, perched atop a column. The room served, the architect said in an article Ford read, as an observation post over the ocean for the owner. The house next to it featured a 3-story wall of glass brick, which cast a dazzling rectangular glare on the sand in front if it, and had been featured in several magazines because of its interior waterfall. In front of these palaces a steady stream of roller skaters zoomed past and around the pay phone at which Ford and Boland stood.

"Hi Nat," Boland said into the phone. "I'm back. There seems to be some kind of problem--"

Ford watched intently as Boland's face went through a series of changes. The metamorphosis from confidence to chagrin was a classic comic routine. Ford wasn't laughing.

"What?" Boland said. "You must be crazy, I--"

"The pilot." Ford nudged him. "Ask."

"No, I certainly did not--" Boland was gesturing with his free hand.

"For God's sake, what's happening?"

"Well fuck you too, then." Boland stood looking at the handle of the phone.

"What?"

"Nat, my agent." Boland said. "That one is the original luftmensh, and he has just announced he is no longer representing me."

"Why?"

"He says he was eating at his special table with some industry people and another agent stopped by and cracked wise that he heard Nat was repping deadbeats these days and everybody laughed. He says this is a small town and he can't afford to represent somebody with serious money problems. Can you believe that?"

"So who'll negotiate for the pilot?"

"Beats me," Boland shrugged. "I'm heading back to the house."

"You're going to have to get somebody else right now on that pilot--"

"I can't believe it. I've been with Nat three years. He said people forget whose the money problem is, just that there is one."

"We can't afford to be without representation at this point--"

"You know, this is total craziness."

135

Boland strode through his house and took a bottle of Scotch out from under the kitchen sink.

"Herb, look," Ford spoke rapidly, "you know I'm on a 12 step program--"

"Yeah, you're a drunk, that's why Diesel got you for next to nothing."

"No, because I used to be a drunk. Why don't you come to a meeting with me? There's one close by, at the Marina, today."

"Because I'm not an alcoholic. I know exactly why I'm drinking, because the whole world has gone crazy." Boland poured a juice glass full of Scotch. "You?"

"No." Ford took out a peppermint.

"Another peppermint?"

"I started when I quit drinking. I suck one when I want a drink."

"You want a drink all the time? You always smell of peppermint."

"I can't help it. I've got an addictive personality."

"I don't."

"Herb, you've got this bill craziness and Diesel's got the tree craziness, and I can't get anybody behind the pilot."

"You know, lately I keep thinking there's a curse on this Plonktown project--"

"I'm driving you up to Diesel's house. We're all going to sit down and get this project moving again."

"—Some kind of weird North Coast Indian spell they put on us because we screwed them up there."

"There was this marvelous movie with Tony Curtis on TV, it was called Manitou, about a dead Indian shaman who came back and killed everybody. The shaman was a succubus on Tony Curtis' girlfriend and he kept growing— the shaman, not Curtis. One of those movies that should have got a lot more attention."

"Thanks, Avery. What I need. A film review."

"I'll call Diesel, find out what time we can see him."

Boland stood at the sink, waiting for the alcohol to hit. The kitchen window faced the back alley and a tow truck flashed its lights, backed in, hooked up his car, and pulled away. Boland didn't move.

He was just beginning a pleasant alcoholic stupor when he turned and walked across the apartment and tripped over a white plastic head in the living room.

"Goddam head from one of Stacy's goddam Pico Tech art courses," Boland roared and kicked at it. He lost his balance and brought his right foot around clumsily to prevent himself from falling, colliding with the heavy Mission Oak footstool, and he broke his toe.

Chapter Eighteen

The rain changed itself into a hissing spray as it hit the sidewalk and bounced up over Henry Richard's shoe. He shivered. He always got a cold when his feet got wet. It was January 3rd according to the **Times Standard** newspaper getting soaked in a rack in front of the Plonktown post office, and that was too early for this kind of freezing rain. The weather logo at the top of the front page showed a cloud with vertical lines coming down on a silhouette of redwoods. It read, "Weather—rain, heavy," but Henry hadn't read the paper. He'd left his gumsole boots at home.

"The City made me change that sign; it wasn't my idea, so the City should put my old sign back the way it was." Henry pointed at the roof of his store.

"The city has no money. I'm going back to the Bank, it's freezing." Eric Linden said.

"That was a fine old sign. I had it for years; it was classic 30's, and those jerks broke something getting it down. I hate that sign they put up there." Henry lifted one foot out of the puddle, then the other. "It keeps reminding me I got taken."

"The city didn't get paid; nobody got paid, so it can't pay you or anybody else. Why are we arguing?"

"I'm not asking the council for the money I'm out of pocket, just for what the city required me to do. I put a $34,000 trust deed on my building, more than anybody else. I don't want to see that phony damn sign every time I walk in my store. And I'm going to take legal action if necessary."

"Go ahead and sue," Linden put up his raincoat collar. "Everybody in town is talking about suing the council, but I can tell you there's no money. There-is-no-money."

"This is a lousy way this city runs--"

"And I'm getting soaked, so if you're through yelling, I don't want to spend my lunch hour here and I'm going back to the bank."

"Bart's right," Henry yelled at Linden's back. "This city has really changed." He shouldered his way through the door

138

of his store and past the reproduction golden oak dining sets he kept up near the front. The style was very heavy and very popular, and Sally was sitting at the end of an oval oak table, sorting through a pile of letters.

"You didn't wear your boots," she said. "The paper said rain."

"Yeah, and every year right after Christmas people around here start looking at the sky and wondering how much water we're going to get this rainy season, and that paper quotes some old local fart who says, 'Yeah, this is the year, I can always tell, this is the year we're going to get floods'."

"What's that? Another bill?" He pointed to one envelope.

"You always do that," she reached for it, "you ask me what's in the envelope before I open it."

"Well, dammit, you can look at the return address--"

"Whoa, honey." She opened the envelope. "Some bank, offering loans."

"Throw the damn thing out. I don't want to hear about any more loans."

"Henry," now she put down the envelope. "What?"

"I want to tell you." Henry walked to the back of the store, poured a cup of coffee from the coffee maker, wrapped his fingers around the cup for warmth, rescued a discarded envelope, put the cup on it, and sat at the table. "I don't know if I can explain."

She pushed away the mail. "Try."

Silence. She reached over and took a sip of his coffee.

"See, I never thought Yancey's idea was going to work. For Tom Harly."

"Well it worked. The kid is weird, but he's smart."

"I thought the kid was blowing his horn; you know, like Tony's kids do all the time."

"Well, that's good, that it worked. Right?" She looked her question.

"Now Marge has a scam. And she's a woman."

"And you went with the guys to talk to Bart about how crazy he's being about her going."

The muted bells signaled the store door opening and Jen Poway came in, wearing a yellow slicker and Wellington boots.

"Early for this rain," she said.

"Gonna be a pisser, this winter, freezing rain starts this early," Henry agreed.

"Hey, Jen," Sally rose, "how you feeling?"

"Not so good today." Jen took off her yellow slicker hat. It made a puddle on Henry's oak table. "I get sick mornings, and it's hard, me being at my sister's."

"Oh." Sally said.

"See, they only have one bathroom."

Henry remained seated.

"And her littlest isn't toilet trained. And that makes me sicker."

"Oh," Sally said again. "Well, what can we--"

"I, uh, I need some, uh, baby things." Jen's face was expressionless.

"For sure," Sally said. "Henry has a catalog on the cutest line; you won't believe how sweet it is. We don't keep the furniture here, but we'll have it in plenty of time for you."

Jen cleared her throat. "I was thinking of a crib," she said, "and one of those tables to change the baby on."

"And you'll need one of those infant car seats." Sally said. "There's a terrific one with a handle in the catalog; you carry the kid on your arm like a basket."

"I, uh, assume you guys do credit?"

"What's your arrangement with Bart--" now Henry rose.

"Credit's fine." Sally said. "Why don't you take the catalog with you and then return it with your order? Henry'll get it. Henry?"

Henry looked at them. Both women looked at him. Sally folded her arms. Henry went behind the counter and handed the catalog to Jen, who tucked it under her yellow slicker and left.

"Why did you do that?" Henry wiped the puddle on the table. "I don't know if Bart is picking up her bills."

"Henry, give her a chance. These people are our friends. Both of them."

"We're already stuck by the film company and now the city won't pay me to put back my regular sign, which the city made me change. I never wanted to change it."

"You're going to take the whole thing out on Jen?"

"The sign company says it will be $7,900 to repair it because all the neon got broken when they took it down. Where do you think the money's coming from?"

"If we took a chance on the film guys, we can take a chance on Jen Poway. At least she's going to be here."

"I like to get paid. This whole thing is because I didn't get paid."

"The Poways are not deadbeats; it's their first baby-"

"Her first, not his first, and maybe he doesn't want to pick up the bills."

"Henry," she pulled out a chair for him at the oval table, "you said you wanted to tell me what's bugging you, but you're not telling me."

He sat down and made a pile of the mail. "See, now Harly's got Yancey's scam and it's working. And Marge has a scam. That means I'm the only dope couldn't figure a way to get back at Boland and Diesel."

"Oh."

"Yeah, oh. And I have to walk under that goddam fake sign on the top of this building every day."

"Henry, we'll buy a new sign--"

"It's not even the money. I figure that's gone."

"I'm sure they'd give you credit for a new sign--"

"And I'm waking up nights and it's eating me and eating me. And I can't think of anything." He looked away from her. "Can you?"

"Well, everybody's doing something they know about, Elwood with the trees, and Bart with the Rolls and Yancey with the computer. So what do we know about?"

"Furniture and art." He was creasing the edges of the envelopes with his fingernail.

They both sat.

"And you know about traveling, from when you were a stew."

141

"Nothing comes to mind," she admitted after a few minutes.

"Exactly," he shook his head, "getting back at those film guys—I figure it's part of healing."

"I already agreed."

"So now I'm sitting around with my $34,000 second and feeling like I got the shaft and there's not a damn thing I can do about it and so help me God, I feel like I've got a grudge against the world."

"Henry, we're smart, you know about things--"

"Compliments," he smiled wryly, "that means you feel I'm really blowing it."

"Henry--"

"I can't get it out of my head."

"OK," she said, "then we have to ask for help."

"Now who in hell am I going to ask for help on something this crazy—"

"I'll tell you."

"I love it! You stick your neck out for once and you get your head chopped off!"

Tony Richard threw back his head and bellowed with laughter, his Adam's apple vibrating above the vee neck of a Hawaiian shirt worn over British officers' shorts. He was sprawled in a swivel chair, his feet in canvas topsiders propped on the wastebasket in his den, long tan hairy legs making him half a foot taller than Henry.

The rest of the den contained two Barcaloungers® in front of the TV set; a plastic armchair; and several shelves covered with magazines. A street map of Las Vegas was framed on the wall. A swag lamp descended from the ceiling, its plastic wire interleaved with a chain, which formed a loop up to a large cup hook in the acoustic ceiling.

"See? I knew you were going to say that." Henry squirmed on the edge of the plastic armchair.

"And now you're stuck with a loan you put on your real estate? You? Old neither a lender nor a borrower be? Wheeee!"

142

"I told Sally talking to you wasn't going to work." Henry stood up and started to walk out.

"Just a minute, little bro," Tony's feet slammed down off the desk and he caught Henry's forearm in a firm grip, stopping him. "I'm entitled to one good laugh."

"I came because Sally persuaded me to see if you had a serious suggestion--"

"Ah, that gorgeous honey, and she's got brains too. She's even got you weaned off polyester, by God. She buying your clothes?" Tony fingered Henry's cotton navy crew neck pullover. "I don't know what in hell she's doing hanging out with you, Henry."

"This is not about my clothes--"

"You haven't asked me yet, have you? I mean, did I miss it? You told me what happened, but did you get to the part where you ask me for help?"

"I asked Sally two days ago and she said I should talk to you."

"You asked Sally? Why didn't you ask me if you should talk to me?"

"It's your attitude. Instead of laughing so hard you'll get a hernia—"

"My attitude? My attitude? How do you think my attitude was all these years being the family fuckup while you were being St. Henry of the Redwoods?"

"I thought I was doing you a favor; I never crowed over you--"

"Ask me, Henry. I'm standing here. Go ahead."

"So then you say there's nothing you can do and fall over laughing. No way!" Henry started for the door.

Tony marched over to a Barcalounger®, sat down, and folded his arms.

Henry stopped at the door. He returned. He closed his eyes. "Will you help me?" his voice sounded strangled. There was no answer. Henry scrunched open his eyes.

"Of course I will," Tony said. "We're not that far from being Ricciardis, remember, just one generation. I can hear pop telling us, 'You boys got to stick together because all you two got is each other.' That's what he kept saying, right?"

"Right." Henry felt for the armchair and sat down.

"And that's what went on when you took over my kids like I couldn't support them, right?"

"Well, I can see you're pissed, but I'm surprised you felt that way because you sure never told me so, and I thought I was helping."

"And when my kids came home and I didn't have any money, as usual, and then they asked me did you have more money than I did because you went to college."

"Tony!" Henry looked at him. "You're right. What I did was wrong." He stood up. "We're not getting any place with this."

"Yeah, we are," Tony waved him to sit back down, "because I'm keeping in mind you did help me when I needed it. So I'm trying."

"And all the times I helped you made you mad? Because you never even thanked me."

"OK, so new game." Tony grinned and broke up laughing again. "So now you're real worked up about this and you want to know, can I help. To take care of this guy, Diesel."

"Right." Henry chewed a hangnail. "Well, it keeps eating at me, aw, Tony, I wake up in the middle of the night having imaginary conversations where I tell Diesel off. It's eating me that he pulled this and I can't think of anything to get back at him."

"So we take care of it." Tony said. "We show him he should maybe have a change of mind about the way he treats people."

"Nothing violent."

"Of course nothing violent, what are we, felons? What do you want to do?"

"I want--" Henry hesitated. "Tony, I know this doesn't sound Christian, but I want revenge. Maybe I should be down on my knees in a church instead of here."

On the other side of the thin wall the baby began to wail. They could hear Tony's wife walking across the room to it, cooing.

Tony considered. "Then it's good you waited this long. Mama had a saying in Italian, 'Revenge is a dish best served cold'."

"What?"

"The best revenge ripens slowly."

"So then what?"

"You have to do it right, no compromise. It's like music. Like, if I do a song, I make it the best I can. It's got to be a work of art."

"But do you know something I can do?"

The baby's screams turned to gurgles as the mother picked it up. A door closed as she carried it to the kitchen.

"A bastard like this," Tony leaned back in the Barcalounger® and crossed his arms behind his head, "you got to get him where it hurts; you understand? You got to embarrass the sucker in a way he'll never, ever forget."

Henry wriggled with pleasure at the idea. "You know how to do that?"

"Oh yeah," Tony said.

Chapter Nineteen

"Diesel's not going anywhere," Marge's voice crackled on the walkie talkie. "He's arguing with the guys planting trees."

"We may as well eat. I told you this was gonna take timing." Elwood Stilton emerged from a screen of cigar smoke in the motel room.

"Timing?" Tom Harly walked over to look out the window. "We've been running hourly checks on Diesel for two days and we never even got a chance at him."

The motel room's only window was an aluminum slider facing the parking lot. The room was a long narrow rectangle with twin beds, walnut laminate furniture, a TV, and a bathroom on the inside wall. It had the peculiar motel smell, new carpet mixed with damp. Harly tried to slide the window open, but the aluminum frame was pitted and bent, with a little white aluminum powder deposit on the corner where the two sides met.

Harly opened the door and stepped out. The occasional trees they'd seen driving west along Santa Monica Blvd. from Beverly Hills disappeared in this section, and concrete parking lots stretched up the block. Most of the structures were commercial and the occasional wood frame house that remained usually sported a sign for some home-based business: washer repair; Amway dealership.

The motel was a yucko stucco box, painted the peculiar anemic tan that was favored for 80% of the stucco in Los Angeles. A black exhaust mark in the motel's front wall bulls-eyed a hole in the stucco made by a car with a long rear overhang. Harly walked around the corner of the building. The rear of the property was fenced by a cinder block wall, also anemic tan, with cement mounded on top and pipes poking vertically up at regular intervals.

Harly sighed and returned inside to watch Bart Poway.

Bart was standing in front of the bathroom mirror, bare chested, his pants open, suspenders hanging down over his dungarees. Many men had hair on their chest, but Bart had hair on his belly; furthermore it was black and glossy, unlike the gray hair on his head. He looked at himself. "Maybe I should get a transplant, belly hair up to my head and head hair to my belly." His kit bag was on the toilet seat lid. He wiped away the occasional rivulet of dye with his heavy forearms. He was dabbing Grecian Formula over his front hair, stopping to consider himself periodically. Finally, he carefully showered away any traces of the dye on his skin; combed his hair straight back and blow dried it, using hairspray so it wouldn't make its usual part.

"If Boland's with Diesel, you think he'll recognize me?" he asked, removing the towel from his face.

"Well," Stilton considered, "you look different. I'll give you that. A lot younger. Maybe I'll try that Grecian stuff myself."

"So what are we going to do for the rest of the day, just sit here with 'Gilligan's Island' on the TV?" Tom asked.

"I got us some stuff to eat." Stilton handed around square white Styrofoam boxes.

"Jesus," Tom said, "cold McDonald's?"

Bart closed his eyes and thought about fishing, because he didn't want to show being nervous from the waiting. He loved to fish. Before he was married he used to keep an aluminum boat upside down on top of his camper, so he could pull over and fish, whenever. He kept an anchor and a blanket, and if the fog rolled in, he'd just stay out overnight.

Sometimes he put himself to sleep now, if he was worried about something at the gas station, pretending he was in his boat, in his blanket, listening to the fog horns, the water rocking him gently. But since the gas station, he was always working. He had to give up the fishing, because when people needed you, they needed you, was the way he figured.

Maybe that was one of the things wrong between him and Jen. She used to come fishing, sometimes, before he had the station.

"We're okay; we still have a couple more days," Henry Richard said.

"Easy for you to say; you just leave Sally to run the store. I had to line up a teaching assistant to cover my classes and I don't know how long he can do that." Tom said.

"We knew we'd have to change the timing as we ran up against stuff," Elwood said.

"Well, it should have been part of the plan."

"How the hell was I supposed to know?" Bart put down his hamburger.

"We can't just sit here forever; I'm going crazy," Tom said. "And Elwood, there's no way I can sleep in this room, much less eat, after you smoke that cigar. We'll have to switch rooms."

"OK, switch. The thing with staying is, we all have work to get back to."

They looked at Bart.

"It's not my fault Diesel hasn't been using the Rolls," Bart protested. "Who figured he was gonna stay at home and watch them plant every damn tree himself? You guys understand?"

"What, understand?" Tom said.

"I don't know." Bart shot a sidewise glance at Tom. "You guys don't always. Understand me."

"Maybe there's something we can do to spook him." Stilton said.

"We can't exactly call up and ask when he's going to drive the Rolls." Tom said. "And we can't show him anybody he's going to connect to Plonktown."

"I'll tell you one thing," Stilton grinned. "The way he's re-fertilizing that place, that bamboo we planted in them trenches ought to start showing within a week."

"I'd love to be there when he finds that out," Tom said. "It'd almost be worth getting ripped off."

Bart tried to stop hearing them. It'd never be the same, him and Jen. Maybe something different between them, but not the same. He was always wondering now, when she wasn't with him, who she was with.

"You sure he won't just have it all dug out?" Tom asked. "I mean once he figures out what it is?"

"Bamboo?" Stilton ground out his cigar. "You try digging out bamboo, son. It puts out runners and goes about 12 feet down. The only way he's gonna get that sucker out is to dig off about the 2 top feet of the whole yard and napalm it."

"Bart," Tom walked over to him, "you're still sort of mysterious about what you're planning when we do smoke out Diesel. You don't have to drag it out. We're all on the hook."

"What I'm going to do," Bart cleared his throat, "is get back my $8,000."

"$8,000?"

"That's what they owe me. For the electricity and the space they rented. I got the bills in from the power company and I sat and added it all up. I'm pretty careful about money."

"What about, uh, other things?" Tom asked.

"First the money," Bart said. "Then I'll take care of the rest of it. You don't understand about the money, because it don't mean the same to you because you didn't get ripped off."

"Yancey got ripped off," Tom considered. "He's a strange kid, quiet. He took my divorce from Sybil hard. Working on this film was one of the first things he did with people in a long time. I don't like it that they bounced his check. It's not the money."

"That's right," Bart nodded. "It's not."

"Then what are you going to do with the $8,000?"

"Funny, because I just now decided about that money." Bart put the Grecian Formula in his kit. "I'm gonna look to put it as the down on a boat."

"And the other thing is, Yancey's mother is on me about his check bouncing." Tom said.

"You got to stop hovering over that boy," Bart said. "Let him be."

"Wait'll you have one." Tom said.

"Yeah," Bart said. "Yeah."

"Jesus, Bart I didn't mean it that way--"

"This is lousy." Stilton stood up and threw his Styrofoam box with its half-eaten hamburger in the plastic trashcan.

"Don't throw food there." Tom stood up. "I'll put it outside in the dumpster."

"Would you leave my garbage alone? You're not staying in this room tonight, right? So just leave my garbage alone."

"What the hell--" Tom put the trashcan down.

"Because I'm getting tired of this holier than thou ecology bit from you all the time. You got that righteous expression. But I know more about the woods than you guys with the books will ever learn. I lived in the woods and made a living there, and one of the things I know is, it takes a certain amount of dirt for things to work. So just leave my stuff alone."

"Elwood, we're all interested in the ecology. I used to smell the water from the mill outfall in the bay, days I went fishing." Bart walked between Stilton and Tom, who stood glaring at each other. "Made my eyes burn. But I know one thing."

"What?"

"I been away from the station now a couple days. Got one of my men running it. So it either gets along some without me or it goes down and I lose it."

"What would you do? After, I mean." Stilton asked. "You're never away from the station. I never even been to your house except that one time."

"Go fishing on the boat I'm gonna buy," Bart said.

"Diesel's got to figure out what's happening," Elwood said. "All this and then stuff going wrong for Boland too. He's gonna figure the odds."

"Nope," Tom said. "He thinks he's untouchable."

"I think we ought to quit for the day," Marge crackled on the walkie talkie.

"Jesus, another night in this motel," Tom complained.

"Why don't you watch the cable?" Elwood asked. "They got the 'Wrath of Khan'."

"Now—quick, he's coming out!" Marge's voice squeaked on the walkie talkie at 8 o'clock the next morning. "And he's driving the Rolls."

"On my way," Tom marked his book, ran outside the motel, snatched open the tow truck door and started the motor.

"Remember to use your right rear mirror," Bart ran out of the other motel room.

"If it all goes really wrong," Henry panted up behind Bart, "I'll be parked on the bottom of the hill, just get on the walkie talkie."

"For Christ's sake, Henry--"

"Piece of cake." Tom reached through the half open truck window and tapped Henry's arm.

Bart tried to attach his suspenders to his jeans, bending backward. "Now it's finally happening I'm scared."

"Gonna go down smooth," Tom rolled the window down the rest of the way. The morning breeze talcumed his cheek with fine dust. His eyes itched. One of the things he missed most in Southern California was early morning freshness.

"Luck," Bart said. He rapped the driver side door with his knuckles.

As he drove out of the lot, Tom could see the three of them in his right rear mirror: Bart, Henry, and Elwood, standing in the parking lot. Tom took La Cienega north to Sunset, watching the early morning bustle: waiters putting out signs listing the specials for the day; shoe stores rolling out pipe racks of women's shoes; produce trucks lined up at the bottom of Beverly Center. He spotted Diesel's Rolls on Sunset Blvd. and fell back a block behind him. He didn't need to be closer. According to their notes on Diesel's schedule, today he was heading for the Harbor Freeway.

Tom was glad to be out of the damn motel, and to tell the truth, glad to be away from Bart. Although how the hell long did Bart expect to keep it secret about Jen, he couldn't figure. It was ridiculous, Jen was five months gone and he didn't know who Bart had told and he worried he'd say something to the wrong person.

He didn't want to think about Bart, didn't want guilt about telling about Jen to get in his way. Because Tom didn't feel scared. He felt exhilarated. He found, to his surprise, he relished being part of the scam, and he didn't want Bart to take down his mood. Maybe he had a flair for acting.

Tom followed the stream of traffic, keeping to the right, and hoping fervently he wouldn't be forced to pass Diesel.

For a mile he concentrated on navigating among the autocides on the freeway, as the traffic thickened.

In the left lane Tom glimpsed two fiftyish men dressed in expensive crew shirts, driving telephone-equipped Mercedes, one behind the other. Except for the crew shirts, Tom thought, they looked like executives. Mercedes 1 picked up his car phone and slowed to 65. Mercedes 2 honked and swerved to his left, into the emergency lane. Mercedes 1 flicked his eyes, still on his phone, and speeded up, just enough to hang Mercedes 2 in the emergency lane. Mercedes 2's driver showed great dexterity in making obscene gestures with both hands while swinging back behind Mercedes 1.

Suddenly the traffic ahead backed up—there seemed to be some kind of tie-up, but a large panel truck was in front of Tom and he couldn't see. He could hear horns.

It wasn't until he inched around the curve that he saw that the tie-up was Diesel's Rolls. Diesel stood outside the passenger door, his arms folded, a furious effort at self-control etching lines on the sides of his mouth. His face was covered with a light sweat.

Tom kicked on the whirling light above his cab and inched left in front of the Rolls.

"Mister," he yelled, "you're in a real bad spot here; they can't see you when they come around the curve. Let me pull you off the freeway."

"Right. I do not believe it; I simply do not believe it."

"Get in the cab." Tom hooked up the tow to the front of the Rolls. Other drivers passed, horns blaring. Please God, Tom prayed, let it hold. Don't let me drop a Rolls on the Harbor Freeway.

"Where do you want me to take it?"

"The Rolls Store," Diesel said, "although why I'm even bringing it there I don't know. I just got it back."

"If it's got random problems, those can be hard--"

"They've got twenty mechanics; I've already paid them several thousand dollars, they tell me it's fine, and none of them can fix a simple problem with the timing on this machine."

"That's over on Olympic? I got a schedule to make."

"Yes." Diesel said. "A Rolls, you're paying a premium for the car. There's a state commission that oversees car repairs. I'm sending them a registered letter with complete copies of my file of bills."

"It'll be $70 for the tow."

"All right. I intend to find the name of the head of that commission and write him personally--"

"Cash."

"What? I don't know if I have cash; I have credit cards."

Tom pulled over to the side of the street.

"No, no, wait, I have it." Diesel was pawing through his wallet.

"In advance."

"All right, all right!" Diesel handed it to him. "I'm ready to have them sell the damn thing. The very idea, to get stuck in traffic like this."

"Calm down now, mister."

"In a Rolls, standing there, watching people. People love to see a Rolls towed; now that just makes their whole day!"

"Rolls Store already tried to fix it?"

"I just told you, they've had it 3 times."

"And it ain't fixed?"

"Well you can see, I mean you can look. Just stalled and the thing would not start, it-would-not-start!"

"Well, if the guy didn't know." Tom shrugged, a minute motion, eyes on the traffic. "With a Rolls, you gotta get somebody knows."

"What do you mean, didn't know? That car has never been touched except by a factory authorized dealership."

"Well, you know how that goes," Tom swiveled a hand, palm down. "The head mechanic's good, but then they turn the car over to some illegal knows how to turn one screw."

"That's infuriating. On top of everything else, I'm late for court, and this is not a judge inclined to take kindly to lapses."

"Top guy on Rollses works out of the Simi dealership, of course, guy name of Bart."

"What?"

"Trains a lot of the Rolls mechanics in town, this guy."

"Well, for God's sake, I'll get him--"

Tom turned his head to look at the side mirror before turning left. "Guy who manages out there, he swears by this Bart."

"Look, pull over to that phone booth on the corner and I'll call Simi."

"Oh, you couldn't get it in over there for maybe two months. They book him pretty solid. And you know they're gonna put the cars they sold first."

"Are you crazy? I can't put up with this for two more months--"

"I heard," Tom lowered his voice, "he does a little moonlighting, Bart, works Saturdays. For cash. Dealership don't know about it; they'd have a fit they knew he was cutting them out."

"As long as he can fix the damn thing--"

"Funny old bastard, Bart, won't say ten words, but like I said, he knows his stuff. He ain't cheap. I'll give you a number you can reach him at."

Diesel flicked his glance back and forth from the Rolls to Tom. "You really think this Bart is good?"

"Mister," Tom pulled up to the Rolls Store's gleaming art deco façade and opened his door, "I promise you, he's the man can fix this car."

Chapter Twenty

Construction of garages in Diesel's Beverly Hills neighborhood was closely regulated by a Community Board of Architectural Review. Diesel's garage was faced with white stucco to match his house, and it resembled a sugar cube, with sculpted arches shaped above the garage doors and high glass brick slots on the street side, through which the sun came into the garage. It parked five cars and had a broad turning area in front paved in square gray cobbles. Bart Poway and Zoltan Diesel were examining the Rolls inside.

Slowly, Bart thought, slowly. Because his hands were wet with sweat and if he dropped a part he'd never convince Diesel. It'd been a while since he'd seen the inside of a Rolls motor except for the one time before in Diesel's garage. They weren't exactly a hot item in Plonktown. A lot of stuff had changed in the motor. Jesus, what if he couldn't fix the damn thing? That'd be a helluva note.

"Be sure you don't scratch that fender," Diesel hovered.

Both Bart's hands were gripping one of the cables under the hood, his body horizontal over a towel spread on one of the fenders. Abruptly, he thrust himself out from under the hood and slid off the fender. He wiped a narrow swath of oil on a rag from his pocket and grunted.

"Well? Can you fix it?"

"Uh, yeah." Bart rocked on his heels. Could he be laying it on too thick? No, he was probably exactly Diesel's vision of a mechanic.

"What's wrong with the damn thing?"

"They had this problem with that model," Poway nodded. "I'll fix it."

"And how much?"

"$8,000."

"Jesus Christ! You must be crazy--"

"Cash," Poway said. "In advance. I supply the parts and do the work right here in your garage. Have it fixed today."

"You're out of your mind--"

"So take your chances." Bart started picking up his tools.

"And cash? Nobody has that kind of cash around--"

"I'll give you one hour," Bart checked his watch, "then I stop working."

"No, you'll wait. I'm going to stand right here. I'm tired of having people working on this car; it hasn't been right since Christmas."

"No way. I ain't giving lessons."

"Now you listen to me, how am I supposed to know if it's fixed?"

"Test drive it." Poway removed some tools from a kit. "When I'm finished I'll go with you while you drive it around. But you bring the money now."

Bart began to hum after Diesel left, his usual off key hum. This really was a beautiful motor; it was a pleasure to work on. Bart did his most important thinking, he'd noticed, when his hands were busy. Work freed his mind to go off someplace and then come back and let him know the decision before he knew he made one.

He was becoming more comfortable with the idea to get out of the gas station business; of course, that would be when this scam was over. Then he'd have time to do things, just regular things—fishing, movies; he used to like movies.

And swap meets, especially car parts swap meets! Jeez, when had he been to a car parts swap meet? He loved going to those. Diesel's garage was a peculiar place to settle the rest of his life. Bart glanced out the garage door.

Because of the curve in the street, he couldn't see Avery Ford shift into low as he drove Herb Boland up the hill to Diesel's house.

"You have to take over," Ford said. "This is the last afternoon I can come up to push Diesel to market the damn Plonktown pilot."

"Got to show the flag--" Boland's voice slurred.

"I have to be in Burbank next week because February 3rd we start Zoltan's new western."

"So I back you up--"

"I have to do it; I can't get any other work. Zoltan's been busy on the phone telling everybody I'm hallucinating."

"Diesel's trying to write the damn western too--"

"So I brought you so you can back me up. Because we need the Plonktown pilot marketed."

"Right, need my work seen too, not in limbo--"

"We need ads in 'TV Guide' and we need public relations. I have some ideas; say a release that one of the girls is going to marry a lumberjack she met during filming. With a picture of the two of them in front of a redwood. Or something about how someone in the cast got scared by a bear when we were filming in the woods last summer. And a picture of a mother bear with her cub. You know the kind of crap."

"What? I didn't see any bear--" Boland's head lolled.

"I can't believe that bastard, Diesel, first his trees and now his Rolls! I think the prick gets his jollies from seeing me plead. So this is my last shot, and after today, forget it."

"Right, I have to take over, concerned about my work too, old reliable--" Boland's elbows fanned out.

Ford looked at him. "People always think they can handle booze, but you're drinking so much I had trouble propping you up in the MG today."

Ford didn't know he almost gave Henry Richard a heart attack down at the base of the hill, where he was hidden.

"It's that actor, Avery Ford, again, and he's got Herb Boland with him!" Henry crackled over the walkie-talkie.

"Jesus," Elwood relayed on the walkie talkie to Tom Harly, hidden near the top of the hill, "every time this Ford shows up. You think he's got something going with Diesel? I hear a lot of these film guys is faggots."

"What'll we do?" Harly asked.

"Tom, you've got to do something to stop him," Marge said from the shrubbery near Diesel's gate, "now."

"Me? What?"

"I don't know, something. It can't be anybody he'd spot. You're the only one he doesn't know. Watch out!"

Harly saw the MG winding up the hill. He waited until it was coming around the curve just below him.

"Hi," Harly stepped out into the street right in front of the MG.

Ford slammed on the brakes, losing Boland, who slid to the floor of the MG in a heap.

"I need four bucks for a drink," Harly said, putting his palms on the hood of the MG for support, "and a ride back down the hill."

"Right," Boland climbed back up to the seat from the floor, "I'll go with you."

"Why me," Ford rolled up his eyes in exasperation. "I've already got one drunk in the car. At least you're direct, no long song and dance like this guy."

"I have a right to drink," Boland declaimed, with an extended index finger. "Do you know, I called the computer outfit pays my residuals. I so-help-me-God Fed Exed them copies of those statements they sent me."

"Herb, don't start--"

"And then I called them. You know what they said? They said there may have been some kind of computer error, but certainly I knew what I earned."

Tom Harly's smile broadened.

"Look," Ford thought the smile was for him, "any other time, fella, but right now I'm in a hurry--"

Tom unfolded himself across the road and lay in front of Ford's car.

"Get up!" Ford yelled. "I swear to God, I'll run you over." He inched forward.

"Just down to Sunset," came Tom's voice, now almost under the front bumper.

Ford put his hand on the shift, unmistakable sign of going forward.

"I hate to insist, but I really am in a bad way," Tom said from below. "You never been there?"

"Sure have," Boland muttered. "I insist on a drink for this man before we see Diesel. I'll have one too."

Ford put his head on his hands on the steering wheel.

"You can't run him over! You want me to go with you, you buy him a drink," Boland pointed to the street in front of the car. "Simple humanity."

"All right, get in. Just to Sunset, mind, and one drink each and I mean it." Ford made room for Tom to perch on the rear of the MG.

An hour later Zoltan Diesel guided the Rolls back from a careful test drive. Bart got out of the car and stood leaning on the door of the garage while Diesel patted the Rolls, his hand lingering.

"Don't worry," Diesel said, "I never complain about money paid for competence. This car is running like it used to. And I've already paid a fortune to that damn dealership for nothing."

Bart nodded, put his kit in the cab of his truck, started the motor, and headed for the gate.

"Hey!" Diesel called.

Bart did not turn off the motor.

"How do I get you if I need you again?" Diesel walked over.

"Ain't gonna need me. When I fix them, they stay fixed. I can guarantee you'll never have that problem again."

"Still, if something goes wrong--"

Bart shifted the truck. "I'm thinking of retiring," he said.

Diesel gaped at him. "Retiring? You can't be forty years old."

"Right, and while I'm young, I'm gonna retire. Actually, I'm going fishing."

"Fishing? I can see you lack the business sense to go with your automotive skills." Diesel's pale lips became tight and stern. "And I can certainly see why the dealership has to look after you. Let me tell you, rationalizing your own failure at business is no solution."

"Is that too much for a man to ask? A little time to go fishing?" The truck pulled out of the gate and Bart picked up his walkie talkie. "Marge, it's over. Get in the road. I'll pick you up as I come down the hill."

Avery Ford drove back up the hill. "Now, you're sober enough to talk to Diesel?"

"Ready and able," Boland revolved his wrist in a circle. Then he revolved his head, stretching his neck.

"Because you've got to explain to him, because he's going crazy—Jesus Christ!" Ford swerved as he almost hit Marge, who had just stepped out of the shrubbery. He jammed to a screeching stop and Herb Boland hit the floor a second time.

"What the hell?" Boland picked his head up above the dash board.

"It's you! Ford screamed. "You're the librarian. You're the librarian from HSU!"

"Uh—no hablo ingles," Marge said. She waved a hand in front of her face and started to walk faster.

"I spent hours in your library--"

"Christ, are you starting that again?" Boland was climbing up on the seat. "You know how Zoltan feels about that librarian crap. I'm telling you, he'll throw your ass off the western tomorrow."

Bart's truck came around the curve and stopped for Marge.

"No, wait a minute," Ford got out of the MG and ran toward the truck.

"Mi novio," Marge said, slamming the door of Bart's truck. "Go!" she hissed.

"What the hell?" Bart gaped at her.

"Go. Now!" she said.

"You," Ford ran around toward the driver's side of the truck, "I know you--"

"Out of here," she screeched.

Bart looked at Ford, screaming, gesticulating, running toward his window. He jammed the truck in gear and pulled around the MG and away.

Ford ran back to the MG and roared into the Diesel estate.

"Who's that?" Ford swiveled his head and pointed after Bart's truck, across the reclining Boland.

"The only competent Rolls mechanic in town, apparently," Diesel replied. "And on top of that, the man's nuts."

"I know I've seen him somewhere before. Herb, do you know him?"

"Can't quite place him," a corner of Boland's mouth curved into a smile. "Can't see too well." Boland dropped his head on the back of the seat.

"You wouldn't believe what he charged," Diesel said. "And in cash. These guys don't pay taxes, of course; it's a real scam. The rest of us pay taxes and they have a cash income which goes straight in their pockets. And then he had the gall to lecture me about fishing. Fishing!"

"What the hell is that?" Ford gaped.

"What the hell's what?" Diesel asked, his eyes still on the Rolls.

"Leaning just inside the garage door," Ford said. "It looks like a big white plastic foot."

Chapter Twenty One

Henry Richard hated to travel.

He hated motels; they made his skin itch.

He hated airports; they confused him and made him feel incompetent.

And he always packed the wrong clothes.

There were three travel agencies in the Humboldt Chamber of Commerce that sent him glossy brochures— Mardi Gras in New Orleans; skiing in Telluride; tours of Napa Valley wineries. He looked at the brochures for the great graphics. But he had no desire to travel.

"But you should travel, Henry," Tom Harly said.

"My friends think it's some kind of character flaw, not wanting to travel," Henry said.

"Well, you should broaden your outlook, see other places--"

"Why? Is it some kind of civic duty? Who says I can't stay home on my vacation, and paint, and go out to dinner with Sally?"

Worse, this was his fourth trip south in the past two months, not even counting the trip to Vegas to see Tony. And he hated to leave Sally alone in the store this long, even though Jen promised to go sit with her.

And what he saw of the San Fernando Valley, that northern suburb of Los Angeles, did not change his mind. People talked about the exuberance of Southern California architecture, the sense of breaking rules. But driving through this neighborhood, the buildings all looked alike: four-story apartment buildings, each apartment with a two-foot-wide balcony with a painted pipe railing, a tribute to the aesthetic taste of some developer fifteen years ago.

"What are those things?" Henry glanced sideways at Tony, who was draped over an overstuffed sofa in a cocktail lounge filled with upholstered seating groups around small tables. The floors were pickled oak covered with dhurrie rugs and the walls were hand-trowelled vanilla colored stucco in a stab at anonymous ethnic. In one corner of the room was the discreet bar, and Henry noticed the waiters combed their hair straight back off their foreheads, unparted, European style. One waiter had a short neat braid in back, but it didn't look like the long scraggly braids Henry had seen on men in Plonktown.

"They're called Little Angels," Tony carefully slit a packet and placed it in the French cuff of his left sleeve.

"What?"

Tony rotated his wrist and admired the diamond cufflink, which winked in the dim light. "Because they make people sleep like Little Angels. Look at these links, aren't they great? Sandra gave them to me for our wedding. Ah, when you're good, you're good."

"You're sure this stuff can't hurt Diesel? What if he gets sick?"

"Nah. We use them at the club where I work. Every once in a while we get a noisy drunk; somebody who makes it crazy for the band, nobody can perform. And if you turn loose the bouncer, sometimes we have to, but some of these drunks are big; it's a real free-for-all."

"Tony, what free-for-all?" Henry swiveled his hips to move to the edge of his chair.

Tony knocked back a Scotch mist and signaled for another. "So what we do is, somebody in the band offers to buy the guy a drink, and puts one of these in it. The drunk goes to sleep, and we pile him in the back room. He wakes up a couple hours later not remembering anything and figures he had a helluva time."

"Maybe you better not drink another--"

"Little bro, in my business, you learn to drink and stay fresh as a daisy."

"We don't even know Diesel comes in here--"

"Yeah, we do. There's a picture of him in here in one of those articles you had."

"But we don't know what day--"

"Yeah, we do. I came in here the other night, gave the bartender $20 and told him I want to meet Diesel because I'm trying to get a gig for the band in one of his flicks. He's gonna intro me, says Diesel comes in pretty much Tuesday nights, which is why we're here tonight."

"You gave him your name? What if the bartender remembers you and tells Diesel afterward--"

"No, no. This is my world and I gotta tell you, Henry, you don't know from this world."

"It seems stupid to use your name--"

"It's his liquor license if somebody passes out here after drinking. He's going to be very, very quiet. In fact, he's going to be grateful to us for taking care of a nasty situation."

"There's no point in taking risks we don't have to take—"

"Henry, how come is it you're forever making the rules, and now you're making rules in a place where you don't know from nothing?"

"Diesel probably won't even come."

Tony sighed. "I could of got one of the band guys to do this, but I figured it's better between the two of us. Maybe I was wrong."

Henry stiffened. "I'll be all right. You know that, Tony."

"He thinks Diesel has a comadre near here because he comes in with a tall blond showgirl type."

"Jesus, my stomach's in a knot. I can't drink this."

"Leave the drink in front of you and eat some of these Japanese crackers they put on the table. And will you stop jiggling around? You break that bottle in your pocket, we'll never get the stuff off you."

"It's him!" Henry grabbed Tony's arm. "The one with the kind of loose trousers, just came in, he's going to the bar."

"Showtime," Tony stood up, shot his cuffs, and glided over to the bar to take a stool next to Diesel.

"This is Tony Richard," the bartender nodded toward him, "has a good combo. Tony, Zoltan Diesel."

"Mr. Diesel," Tony flashed the dazzling grin, "what a pleasure. I've been trying to talk to you, send over a tape of the stuff we do, maybe for one of your films."

"I'm not looking at anybody for music right now." Diesel tilted his head and stared down his nose.

"Couldn't hurt to listen to a tape, keep an open mind, right? I do the good old songs, and you can see it in the phrasing, the music backs up the meaning of those great lyrics. You're gonna love this tape."

Diesel considered. "Could you work with a girl singer?"

"Of course. We've got some wonderful 30's blues," Tony nodded, "no problem."

"Send the tape to my office."

"I'll put on the outside, 'Requested' so you'll know we talked about it." Tony signaled the bartender.

"I don't know--"

"What could it hurt?" Tony opened his palms.

"All right, I'll listen, but I'm not promising anything."

"Marvelous," Tony smiled, "bring us a fresh round," he said to the bartender.

"I don't want another, I'm on my way someplace--"

"Hey, a little celebration, right?" Tony shrugged. "Let me tell you real quick some things we've done."

Henry watched from the couch.

The bartender delivered the drinks and walked over to switch on the TV, which came on full blast. Everybody glanced up before the bartender raced over and turned down the volume.

"Goddam," the bartender muttered, "cleaning guy's been fiddling with the set again."

Tony raised his glass and clinked lightly with Diesel, who checked his watch and drained his fresh drink. Tony continued to talk, gesturing, chattering about music styles.

"It's not working," Henry said. "I knew this wasn't going to work. Diesel's just sitting there."

"What's not working?" One of the straight-haired waiters asked.

"Uh, the air conditioning." Henry said.

"Well, it is February," the waiter said. "Can I move you to another table, sir?"

Henry looked at the waiter. Waiters in Humboldt County tended to be overweight and cheery, but all the waiters here had trim bellies in their pleated pants. Henry patted the slight protuberance of his own belly. And they had muscular chests under their short white jackets and they all looked tanned and fit. And they all had even white teeth.

Where did they find so many fit waiters? Maybe they picked their waiters off the Nautilus equipment at a local gym.

And Henry was wearing his good dark blue suit because Tony said they'd be at a restaurant.

"No," he said, "this table's fine."

Suddenly Diesel sighed, "Don't understand it—don't feel--" and dropped his glass, which fell over on the bar. His eyes rolled up and he collapsed off the bar stool.

Tony stepped in to catch him before his head struck the bar. Henry walked over to stand beside Tony.

"What the hell is this?" the bartender ran over.

"Don't worry, we can testify he only had two drinks here." Henry said.

"What testify?"

"In the bar across the street, they said the Alcoholic Beverage Commission is checking the neighborhood."

"Jesus," said the bartender, "can you believe my fucking luck? I've never seen the guy drink more than two drinks."

"Well, that's two in this place." Henry said.

"What the hell am I gonna do with him?" The bartender ran back around the bar.

"Maybe we could move him." Tony looked around. You got a back room?"

"Yeah," the bartender nodded. "Look, do me a favor, get him back there."

"I don't know, guy might upchuck." Tony looked at Diesel. "Fifty bucks?"

The bartender looked at him. "Always the goddam squeeze. Okay, okay." He took five bills out of the cash drawer. "Wait a minute, here's the key."

"Take his legs." Tony pointed with his head. "I'll get the arms."

Henry puffed behind Tony to the back room.

"Right here, on these sugar sacks. Nice and comfy."

"What do we--"

Tony held up his hand, listening for the bartender. He took the key from his pocket and locked the storeroom door from the inside. Then he took off his jacket and hung it on the corner of a shelf, carefully tying the diamond cufflinks in the corner of his handkerchief, which he put in the pocket of the dinner jacket before rolling the French cuffs up to his elbows.

"You get him on his back and take down his pants." Tony said.

"What? For God's sake--"

"And his shorts. Well, do it!"

Henry gingerly complied. When Henry rolled him on his back, Diesel began to snore gently.

Henry stood over the half nude Diesel. "Jesus," he caught Tony's elbow, "if somebody walks in now--"

"Shut up." Tony shook off Henry's hand. "Just hold his legs apart." Tony bent over Diesel. "And hand me the Mercurochrome."

"And for God's sake, don't rub him by accident," Tony added. "We sure as hell don't want it to come up."

Chapter Twenty Two

"I don't see why you couldn't call me." Naomi Van Owen slipped the burglar chain on the front door of her town house to let Zoltan Diesel in. She was almost 6 feet tall with a dancer's long-legged body, clad in high heel sandals and a flowing dress which clung to her, no bra, small nipples poking. She was a head taller than Diesel. The surprise was, she was wearing glasses and her green eyes had the soft wet look of myopia.

"Get me some water. I just stopped for one minute at that bar on Parthenia, and I passed out!" Diesel held on the door jamb.

"I couldn't think where you were." Naomi whirled, straight blond hair flicking, and walked across the peach carpet, a dancer's walk, toes out.

"I can't understand it. That's never happened to me before." Diesel followed her into the living room.

The town house was built on four levels. The living room was on the entrance level, separated by a glass sliding door from a patio. The dining room and kitchen were five steps up, overlooking the living room. A stairway doubled back up to a den over the living room, and another five-step stairway led to a huge master bedroom and bath, over the kitchen and dining room.

Naomi dropped on the white sectional sofa in the living room, fronted by a triangular cocktail table covered in peach laminate. "I came home early from rehearsal, just so I'd be here. The bar could have called me; they know my name. At least I'd know what was happening."

"Where's the water?"

"Glasses in the sink in the kitchen," she tilted her head in that direction.

Diesel held tightly to the banister going up. "And then I woke up in this filthy back room, and I didn't know where I was."

"Well, for heaven's sake, why did you go in the back room?"

"I didn't go there, dammit, somebody put me there."
Diesel gulped and splashed water down the front of his shirt.

"Well, anyway, it's over now," she said. "Whatever."

Diesel drank more water.

"Honey, did I tell you they decided Frank and me can open the new revue at the club?" she said. "We're dressed in Spanish outfits; there's some kind of a Mexican festival this February. And they're backing us up with a bunch of mariachis. I think it should be pretty good."

"I could have had a simple reaction to the stress I've been under with the trees."

"Zoltan," she rolled up her eyes, "please, let's not start with the trees." She stood and walked up the stairs to the den level.

"Well, it has to be the stress. First some clown cuts my trees; then we spend weeks and can't find who ordered the tree service; then the Rolls starts acting up." Diesel followed her, the glass of water in one hand, holding tight to the railing.

"I had Ragazzi's send over those shrimp you like; they cost a fortune and now they're like little rubber shrimp from being kept hot. If you want them, they're on the kitchen counter."

"And then I told the bartender to call a taxi because I didn't want to drive and he gave me a whole crazy tirade about his liquor license, of all the goddam things, so I just left and walked here."

"Incredible. I mean, people can be so insensitive." She walked up to the bedroom level, motioning to him to get the light switch. She passed a storage wall faced with white laminate, with shelves, drawers, a TV and a stereo.

"To pass out like that, I never had anything like that happen. You think it could be something serious?" He followed her.

"Of course not, look at you, you're in fantastic shape."

"You think I have a temperature?" He examined himself carefully in the door of the mirrored closet.

"My poor baby." Naomi removed her dress over her head and carefully put it on a hanger, her feet moving across the art deco pattern of a mauve Chinese rug. "I was real worried."

She dropped on the bed. Her bed had a soft sculptured headboard shaped like a shell in sea green and a hand painted spread in which the flowers were outline quilted. The bed was lit on both sides by cylindrical torchiers which focused their soft light on the ceiling. On one side of the bed was a table with a round blue glass top and curved reeded legs, ending in brass plated feet.

"The only thing I don't like about the new Mexican number is, the stage manager has us kiss in one part in the middle, and that Frank's a real gay caballero, if you know what I mean, so who knows what he's got." She put her eyeglasses on the table.

"Funny, Walter was just saying the other day something about illness being the big stick that gets your attention. He's sure right."

"And I told him if he puts his tongue in my mouth I'd deck him right in the middle of the opening number."

"What?" Diesel asked. "What the hell are you talking about?"

"Frank in the opening number—oh, never mind." She removed her panty hose, revealing a long slender body with a uniform tan except for a light bikini line. She rose, nude, and put her high heel sandals in the closet and dumped the panty hose in a hamper. On the wall above her bed were framed photos of her in various magazine ads and two close-ups of her face, and her eyes swept them briefly before she got in bed.

Diesel walked into the bathroom and leaned across the tan marble double sink toward a floor to ceiling mirror which flanked it on three sides. He saw himself infinitely receding in both directions, spotlighted above a surface filled with perfume and cosmetic bottles. He stuck out his tongue and examined himself critically, but he couldn't see any changes. He moved a jar to lean in closer to the mirror.

"Don't mess around with my cosmetics. I like to know just where everything is."

"I can't see anything wrong." He pulled down his lower eyelids. "My eyes are a little red."

"Well of course there's nothing wrong with you."

"I'll make an appointment with a doctor first thing tomorrow to get a complete workup." He walked into the bedroom. "A good internist, I think, to start."

"It's just one of those weird things; maybe you're allergic to something--"

"Maybe it's high blood pressure. They call that the silent killer, and one of the symptoms is you pass out suddenly."

"Come here," she lay back and raised one knee. "I'll take care of the blood pressure."

"I don't know if I should," he said. "Until I find out, that is."

"Oh, come on." She purred. "It'll make you feel a lot better."

"All right."

"Dr. Naomi's personal cure." She arched her back like a cat, stretching her arms overhead and wiggling her fingers in a come hither.

Diesel walked to the opposite side of the bed and dropped his clothes in a heap.

"You can hang your clothes in the closet."

"I told you before, stop worrying. I won't buy clothes that wrinkle."

"See, it's working already." She brought down her arms in a circle around his head.

"The thing is, fainting like that, it was really scary--"

"We'll just take care of that." She unclasped her arms, rolled her tongue around her lips, and lowered her head toward his crotch.

"I really think it's a simple stress reaction--"

"Jesus Christ!" She screamed. "What's that?"

"What's what?" He sat up abruptly. "What do you mean, what's that?"

"That." She pointed. "Are you wearing a red condom? Or are you bleeding?"

"Oh my God!" He yelled, looking in the light of the torchiers at his penile shaft, erect and a vibrant red.

"Call 911," he gasped. "What could it be?"

"Not here," she said. "I want you out of here."

"But you've got to call emergency--"

"Right now. There's all kinds of crazy diseases in this town and I'm not fucking somebody sick."

"But I can't leave this way--"

"I'm very careful about my health. Put your pants on." She leaned to pick them up, then hesitated. "You pick them up." She pointed.

"I thought you said you weren't worried about this." He stooped to put on his jockey shorts.

"Zoltan, when you go to the hospital, don't tell them you were here," she said. "Just tell them you came right from that bar on Parthenia."

"Oh fine. What do I say, 'Hey guys, I have this little problem I have to ask you about'—is that how I start?"

"There's absolutely no reason anybody needs to know you were at my place."

"I actually arranged a meeting with a band for you earlier tonight. God, I can't believe I did that."

"Forget it."

"This is crazy, wait." He half squatted and rubbed himself vigorously, knees akimbo. "There's nothing wrong except the color--"

"Put your pants on. I don't wanna know." She kicked them over with her toe.

"And good night."

Chapter Twenty Three

Henry Richard's house in the forest was in the Pickle Hill section of Plonktown, named for a pickle bottling factory that existed there in the 1930's. The section was described as either "marginal" or "rapidly appreciating" by local realtors, depending on whether they were representing the buyer or the seller.

The original pickle factory was on the river, with a dock to receive shipments of cucumbers, so Henry's land commanded a sweeping view of the Mad River. Henry had bought two ramshackle houses on the next lot, which he converted into rentals, doing the carpentry himself to remove part of the roof, adding skylights, putting in sleeping lofts and wood burning stoves. Since then, the property had doubled in value.

Henry and Sally were working in Henry's studio. The statue of Josiah Plonk was on its back on a wood door which Henry had placed over four wood barrels to raise a table of the right height to work without back strain. The wood door groaned occasionally as Henry bore down on the statue. The smell of solvent was so pungent that one of the windows was propped open in spite of the damp February cold, and Henry and Sally were both wearing old ski jackets.

Now the statue looked like it was in two sections: a clean dull brown for the body, and a weathered blackish green from its knees down. Occasionally Henry's goggled eyes met Sally's goggled eyes across Josiah's shinbones as they both rubbed.

Marge arrived, wearing denims and a fleece-lined coat.

"Sally, that was a great idea, I love it, making those molds from parts of Josiah's statue."

"The molds aren't hard to do." Sally said.

"—And then leaving them around for Diesel and Boland."

"That was not Sally's idea." Henry lifted his goggles. "It was my idea. I was an art major, and I'm the one knows how to make latex molds."

"Well, whoever—"

"And I have ideas too. Leaving the parts of the statue was my idea."

"Whosever idea it was--"

"No, because you and Sally are into this feminist thing," Henry drew himself up to his full five feet six inches," "and that bugs me."

"I didn't mean--"

"It wasn't just Elwood and Bart who got back at those film guys; they bellow and make everybody help them. I had a great scam too."

"Come on, Henry--"

"And it was my idea to leave the plastic statue parts like a calling card. And I resent you saying it was Sally's. You think I couldn't get an idea?"

Silence.

"Did you get to the foundry mark yet?" Marge awkwardly changed the subject.

"A couple more inches," Henry said. "Should get to it in an hour or so."

"So what we're doing in my Art History Class," Sally's eyes flicked under her goggles from Marge to Henry, "is taking rubbings of the headstones at the Catholic Church cemetery on 16th Street."

"The gravestones are Art History?" Marge asked.

"Sure, that church dated from the 1860's, when Plonktown had a lumber boom, and my teacher says it looked like the iconic New England church, white clapboard siding, tall pointy steeple, gothic windows, except all made of redwood, which made it real Pacific North Coast, like the town of Mendocino. Now the church is gone, of course. Blew over in a windstorm. But the cemetery's there."

"Watch, make sure you're rubbing Josiah's leg evenly," Henry pointed, "some of the bronze is worn thin, and if you go through it we've got a major problem."

"It's the only cemetery I've ever seen," Sally gestured with her rag, "organized by country of origin."

"What?"

"Yeah, you should go there, Marge, it says on every headstone, 'here lies so and so, a native of the Azores' or 'so and so, a native of Scotland,' stuff like that. And they're all together; the Italians together, the Portuguese together. You can see where the original muscle to build Plonktown came from."

"There's still a lot of Portuguese up here," Henry tilted his head. "They keep to themselves. A realtor told me that when they buy houses, they buy for cash. They don't believe in loans. If I was Portuguese, see, I wouldn't have that second trust deed on the store."

"The Italian headstones have oval frames with photographs of the person buried, set right into the stone. And there's a whole section with a fence that has a sign says the Serbo-Croatian Society takes care of it, and the headstones there are in the Cyrillic alphabet, because there was a big group of Serbs here." Sally stopped rubbing.

"Pay attention to Josiah." Henry pointed.

She stepped back and cocked her head. "He looks like he's got on fishing boots."

"My boot is shorter than yours. Sally, we're not going to have Josiah ready to go back up for the plaza reopening ceremony unless we really work."

"I ran out of the stuff."

"Go mix some. And watch out you don't splash solvent gunk on my latex molds over by the wall."

"I'm leaving, you're mixing more of that gunk," Marge said. "It gets in my throat and I choke and then I gag."

"I think you ought to make Elwood give you some kind of civic award or citation for doing this," Sally said, after Marge left. "You've spent hours cleaning Josiah, and it's terrible work."

"Can't you just see the citation?" Henry lifted his goggles. "He'd write, 'To the little twerp.' "

"Henry," her voice was a two note, the second note dropping, "that's exactly what I mean. I want some public acknowledgement in Plonktown of what you've done."

"It's enough you think I'm great."

"I want more, after what you've done."

Henry paused before putting back the goggles. "Those guys have taught me some stuff; all this business with

175

Diesel. I couldn't have done most of the scams without them."

"And they couldn't do the latex molds for the statue parts." she tossed her head. Then she had to straighten out her goggles. "So I don't see where that argument gets you. Not to mention you had a scam without them."

"Yeah, well, that one was Tony's idea."

"It counts for you."

"See, everybody scored back at the film company in his own way," Henry said, "so I don't feel like I should get any special recognition."

"Okay, so then I'll ask Elwood for the citation. For me."

"Woman, ah want you to leave me some peace," Henry did a wickedly accurate Elwood imitation.

"Jesus," Sally looked at him, "you're beginning to sound like the guys around here."

"You just want a plaque to show when your girlfriends ask why you married me."

"No," she shrugged, "I just tell them you're great in bed."

"What?"

"Yeah, I tell them you're old enough to have this marvelous control, last longer--"

"Sally!"

"No, I didn't tell them," she said. "But it's true. How about we take a break?" she leered and wriggled her eyebrows.

"Sally, please, we have to work." He put his goggles back on. "I was supposed to get the base finished tonight while Marge was here because I'm going to give her a copy of the foundry mark. You can't see it with all the weathering."

"What for?"

"There's some kind of federal grant money; they're trying to make a master list of all the W.P.A. art in public places: you know, that government agency that hired all the artists in the Depression. We for sure want Josiah's statue on the list."

"The government doesn't know where the W.P.A. art is?"

"Nah, a lot of it's lost, apparently nobody kept an accurate list. And some of those artists became famous and now their stuff is on Post Office walls and outside city buildings and nobody knows it."

"With the Depression, I guess they had other things on their minds."

"Hey, look at that, above the foundry mark. There's a sculptor's signature coming up." He rubbed fiercely. "That's interesting—lot of W.P.A. sculptors didn't sign their stuff, only the best ones did."

"So who is it?"

"It's a small signature, not flourishing. Guess that's why I didn't notice it before. Come on, give me that new gunk you mixed." He bent closer. "Sally, bring me that desk lamp and shine it here."

"H," she bent over it, "Hoff—Hoff something. Hoffman?"

"Sally," he put down his solvent and sat down. "Jesus, Sally, the damn statue is signed by Malvina Hoffman!"

"Malvina who?"

"Malvina Hoffman, dammit!" He bellowed. It was so uncharacteristic for him to yell she almost dropped the lamp.

"What are they teaching you in that school?" he roared. "She sculpted the Races of Man for the Field Museum in Chicago; one hundred and five super-size bronzes; mind you, this was 1933, it was so much work the Museum expected her to hire five other sculptors, and she did it all herself."

"But Henry, what would somebody like her be doing in Plonktown?" Sally sat next to him.

"Wait a minute," Henry was pacing in a circle, "the timing's right, it's right, by God, because she spent time on the West Cost studying the American Indian before she did the Races of Man for Chicago and she worked on the Hearst estate. That'd put her out here right around the correct time—she probably picked up a quick commission in California."

"You mean she's famous?"

177

"Of course she's famous, dammit—she was this maverick sculptress, she wrote books on how to sculpt they're still using in art schools. Her friends were the people in that California Arts and Crafts movement and she believed in sculpture in harmony with nature. Sally, you better get out of the damn cemetery and into the library."

"Just because I didn't hear of her--"

"Where's my book on 20th Century sculpture, I'm sure I have a picture of her in one of my books; there's gotta be a chronology." Henry threw off his gloves and goggles and flipped frantically through one of the books from his bookshelf. "Here, here she is. See, she was Rodin's pupil when she was young. She had this long life, almost 80; died in 1966."

Sally looked over his shoulder at a sepia photograph of a young woman seated on the shoulder of a gargantuan figure, eighty feet in the air on the façade of a building. The woman straddled the shoulder in an ankle length skirt.

"Hey, it says she learned to rebuild tools, bend iron, saw wood, chase and finish bronzes." Sally read over his shoulder. "She must have been some lady." Sally took the book and sat down.

"But even if she did a commission in California," Henry frowned, "how the hell did Plonktown get her?"

"I'll bet I know," Sally's voice was excited. "It was probably because she was a woman."

"Aw, honey, don't start with that crap."

"No Henry, now just listen. It says right here, 'There was no historical tradition of women in sculpture. Ivan Mestrovic, the great Yugoslav sculptor, advised her to overcome this disadvantage by becoming a better technician than the men."

"I told you she was great on materials--"

"See, Henry, I always wondered about that story about the statue. That it was originally for another town up the hill, but the truck delivering it broke down, so the truck driver just left it and that's how come the statue's here."

"What has that got to do--"

"Don't you see? They wouldn't have dared to do that to a top male sculptor, not even in the Depression. But if she was up against that kind of prejudice, it would make sense. They didn't think much of the sculpture and the sculpture looks pretty good to me, even with all the crud. But a woman? Women should be grateful their work got put anywhere, and not complain."

"Oh, now you're interested, because you think she was a feminist? This after you didn't even know she was a sculptress?"

"I may not have known before, but I'm telling you why Josiah's here."

"Look, you realize what this means?" Henry felt along the bench and dropped down.

"It means Marge is going to have an attack—ooh, I've gotta call her, where's the phone?" She burrowed under the drop cloths.

"Not to Marge," he bellowed, "to Plonktown!"

"Well, I can see you're all excited," she came up out of the drop cloths, "but to tell the truth, I don't see why it makes such a big difference. I mean, it's nice to know, but it's the same sculpture, and it's going back in the same place."

"It's not the same. It'll never be the same."

"You really mean it." She dropped on the bench beside him.

"Get me a paper and a crayon. I'm going to make a rubbing of that signature."

"What for?"

"Josiah's statue is going to raise hell among art historians, because it's such an extraordinary addition to her known work. Apparently they had no clue about Josiah existing."

"They won't try to take him away, will they?"

"A major piece of art turns up like this out of nowhere, scholars really descend on it to try to trace the route back, figure where it belongs in her development."

"You mean they'll come here?"

"You bet. We've got a major piece of sculpture on our hands in Plonktown."

"So what do we do now?"

"I guess we start," he crossed his ankles and swiveled his feet, staring at his work boots, "by telling Marge to get hold of the W.P.A. art location project. Then we better call Elwood. Then we better call the newspapers."

"The papers in Eureka?"

"The papers in San Francisco."

Chapter Twenty Four

The marina in Trinidad, about 20 miles north of Plonktown, is at the end of a drive down a steep hill, with wooden houses perched in horizontal steps paralleling each dogleg in the road, and the fishing boats visible as you drive down.

It's a workaday marina, with a small booth at the end for the State Fish and Game inspector, and a huge flatbed scale to weigh the catches from the commercial fishing boats. The dock is made of heavy timbers and is notched so it can be taken in each November and reconstructed each March, because no dock can withstand the crashing tides of the winter storms at Trinidad. A hundred feet out into the water from the end of the dock stands a rock shaped like a seventy-foot-high tooth; its sides covered with brown sea lichen and the droppings of birds. Locals rate the winter storms by how far above the tooth the waves break.

The Portuguese called the port La Santissima Trinidad, the Holy Trinity, and they were still in Trinidad, descendants of the fishermen who came over from the Azores in the last century. At the end of every May they had a procession. They took the statue of the Virgin out of the small white Catholic church at the top of the hill, and they dressed a teenage girl in a ball gown with a heavy velvet cape to represent the Portuguese Queen Isabella, and they got other girls to be her court, and the school band played and they carried the pennants of their religious societies, flapping in the sea breeze. And tough knotty-looking men with moustaches walked the statue of the Virgin on a platform on their shoulders down to the dock to bless their fishing boats.

Sometimes the Virgin was generous. But there was a monument at the head of the hill which said simply, 'Lost At Sea', four flat sides with names. Several women's names were there. Some of the fishing boats were mom and pop operations. Some family names were repeated three or four times, with different first names and years of death. Family members with the same name walked to work each day to the dock, past this reminder of their forebears.

181

"So then you'll be leaving?" Jen Poway sat in the sun on the dock and braided her hair.

"Guy here will give me a good price on this boat." Bart's voice was muffled. He was upended in the motor compartment of a boat, his head and shoulders hidden. Gas fumes blended with the strong smell of fish from the stone cleaning sinks on the dock. The dock around Jen had almost disappeared under the rancid detritus he had removed from the boat, which was now tied to the pilings ten feet below her.

She noticed the left hip pocket of his coveralls was torn up one side. She'd need to mend it. Then she remembered.

"He's been having a bitch of a time with the shaft." Bart continued. "It may be bent and he doesn't know what to do with it and got hisself stuck out on the water last week. So he's fed up. I figure I can fix it."

"If it's machinery, you'll fix it." There was no doubt in her voice. "Motors do that for you. The shaft will probably straighten out just because it knows you're around."

"Anyway, I figure to be gone about two months, go up to Alaska. I got all my licenses and my salmon punch card."

"Uh huh."

"I'll find a mooring when I come back. Summers, Trinidad's better than Eureka Bay."

Jen worked a splinter off the dock.

"Eureka Bay, now, everybody looks at that bay and thinks it's so big it must be a great harbor. But there's a big sand bar in the middle, so you get turbulence in the middle of nowhere, because the tide going out fights for space with the bay water. Lousy for small boats."

The gulls cawed as a fisherman gutted his fish at the stone sink on the dock and threw them his leavings.

"Lots of people go up on the hill behind Eureka and watch with binoculars during storms, see the boats rev up and try to catch a wave and surf over that damn sand bar, try to get in the harbor."

"Why would people want to watch that?" Jen stopped braiding and frowned.

"Well, the boats usually make it."

182

"You could look for a mooring south of Eureka."

"That's a good idea. I been thinking about down at King Salmon. I could buy a lot there cheap, put a mobile home on the lot right next to where I tie up the boat; those canals down there are deep. Of course, now," he looked up at her, "you'll get a check every month from Sam over to the station." He wiped his wide brown hands on a rag, but the blunt nails stayed black with motor grease.

Jen put a barrette on the end of the braid.

"I'm selling him the station, but he had to guarantee you $1500 a month off the top until he pays it off, which will be a long time, and then you'll get a percentage of his gross over that. So you'll be fine."

"I have enough money."

He climbed the ten steps of the worn wood ladder and stood next to her, hands on his ample hips. "What a day, huh? Water sure looks good. I had this thing together, I'd take you for a run."

"You're more like you used to be when we first got together." She glanced at him. "Less—I don't know, less frantic."

"It felt good to pull this Rolls thing off on Diesel." Bart nodded. "I planned it and I did it. Made me feel less stupid."

"Bart, come on, you been running the station for years, helping people with their cars in emergencies, when they're stuck, when they're crazy. Where'd you get this idea about you being stupid?"

"It's just, working all the time like I been—it's all right long as you don't stop and figure out what in hell you're doing with your life. When I stopped, to do this Rolls thing, I got to wondering where's my life."

"So anyway," he tried to clean the black fingernails on a rag, "you remember you was telling me about intensity? That Boland lived on a different level of intensity than we do?"

"Bart, sometimes I get crazy--"

"What I'm saying is, now I know what you were talking about. When I was working with the other guys' scams, and when the Rolls thing went right, I felt—alive. Like I'd been dead. Like I was different. Maybe because I was scared I'd get caught."

"I'm sorry I told you guys the scams wouldn't work."

"I dunno, maybe I made myself numb for a long time so I could work so hard at the station. Thing is, you make yourself numb, then you can't get alive when you want to. Do you understand any of this?"

"I understand all of it. I--" she made a strangled sound.

"Jesus, Jen, what--"

"Bart, this boat—that's like us. With a boat you follow a compass to get where you're going and sometimes you see you've gone off direction. But you don't just give up, you get back on direction and keep going."

"Jen, what in hell are you talking about?"

"I may as well say it. I don't want us to split up."

"Jen, I don't know. I don't think I could be the same."

"We can't know until we try. It's worth a try. Eight years together, what is that, nothing?"

"I trusted you--"

"Look, if we're gonna tell the truth, you didn't trust me. You ignored me. I was just there, like water in a faucet."

"Well, that's sure changed. Now I'm always thinking about who you're with."

The gulls finished the fish leavings and flapped away.

"You mind telling me," he asked, "why that flake, Boland?"

"Bart, he was around."

"I dunno." He shook his head. "The thing made me maddest was you telling me, flat out like that, about Boland. Madder than even you sleeping with him. I felt like you wanted to kill me."

They had eight years of history, so they were quiet. They could tell at a glance when it was best to back off, accept a compromise. They had learned after eight years of arguments and stony silences.

The winch on the boat launch screeched and a large boat started down the concrete runway parallel with the pier. Men shouted directions, children ran to watch; birds flew around.

The boat hit the water and filled the air with coughing and gasoline fumes.

"Don't you think it's funny?" Her face was pinched. "I thought I was being honest for once."

"Jen, look, I don't read all those books, so all I can tell you is how it felt coming at me."

"I went with Herb because I thought he was alive, and it turned out he had been dead so long he was on automatic, reciting the words, like some kind of tape."

"Jenny--"

"See, what he said sounded good to me because he'd practiced it so often. He'd never understand sticking with the same person eight years. He sort of lives in scenes, like movies."

"I don't want to hear about Boland." He balled up the rag and threw it in a trash barrel.

"And meanwhile, now you're alive. You're, um, talking to me. You know? Sort of, we had got to where all we talked about was, did you pick up the potatoes at the store, stuff like that. I didn't know you still felt like this about fishing."

"I didn't know I still felt like fishing. But now I'm not going to forget. I mean, I may stop fishing after two months, do something else. But what I do—I want to get some feeling out of what I do."

"God must have a sense of humor." Jen took a Kleenex® out of her pocket and touched it to the corners of her eyes.

"Jenny, maybe it's me, but are you speaking English any more? Because I don't--"

"I don't know! I don't know what I'm speaking and I don't care. Whatever I'm speaking, nobody listens to me since you moved out."

He looked at her.

"Little things keep happening I want to tell you about, because nobody else cares but you. I hate living alone. Marge likes it, she told me she likes being able to walk around the house in the middle of the night and fart if she wants to. And Sally's been on her own since she was fifteen. But it doesn't work for me. Last night I read a John Grisham

185

novel while I ate dinner; it was better than looking at the wall. And at my Cousin Celia's wedding reception, after dinner everybody at the table danced and I got left playing with the foil from the champagne, nobody to talk to. And I can't--" her voice cracked again.

"Jesus, Jen, I don't know what you want--"

"Sally and Marge think I'm dopey, and I'm all alone, because this independence business doesn't work for me. Because they're them and I'm me. And when I think about you, that's what I miss. My friend." She opened and closed her mouth, but no voice came out.

"Look, just tell me—tell me what you want."

"You got me up at 8 o'clock this morning to see this boat. You were like you used to be, alive like you used to be, and I came before I even combed my hair, and I thought—I thought you meant we were going to be together. On the boat." She shuddered.

"You thought we were getting back together?" His mouth was open.

"Oh my God," she was mopping her eyes with the Kleenex®, "if one person thinks things are better and the other doesn't, that means things are bad before you even start trying to get back together."

"Jesus, Jen, I don't know."

"Uh, okay, so we'll have some problems. I'm not gonna argue with you about that, it's not going to be that easy. But we had problems before. And I want to be back with you."

"Jenny, are you crazy?" he stared at her. "You're due in two months. Remember?"

"So?" she lifted her chin. "You figure my belly's gonna be too big to fit in the cabin?"

They laughed then, the first real laugh for months, so hard they had to put their arms around each other and hold each other up. Children standing on the bank stopped playing and stared, because even young children knew grownups don't laugh like that.

"But what if you have the baby while we're at sea--"

"Wouldn't be the first kid," she shrugged. "There are doctors on the short wave. Give some doctor something to tell his kids."

They laughed again.

"You don't care what the others say?" she gasped, when she could talk. "About the baby?"

"In the middle of the North Pacific? People thought we were doing fine when we were doing lousy. So now they'll think we're doing lousy, and who cares?"

"I've missed you. Christ, I've missed you." She reached out to him.

"So what do you want to do with the house? I mean, I thought you'd finally have the money to do that bathroom you wanted--"

"Lock the door. When we come back, if we don't want it, we'll sell it."

He took her hand to help her down the ladder, then circled her with his arms as she climbed down to the boat. "Look, you're gonna have to make a list of stuff we need."

"Bart, I'll try again, after this baby, to have one of ours."

"This one's ours." He said. "And for Christ's sake, watch your step. You're big as a balloon."

Chapter Twenty Five

"I don't care if you are being married; that damn truck is blocking my driveway and the maid can't get in. Get it moved." The heavyset man jerked the knot of his tan bathrobe.

"I'm not being married--"

"And this is supposed to be a quiet neighborhood and it's Sunday morning."

"Nobody, absolutely nobody, is being married. There's some kind of mistake." The dry bare earth of Diesel's front yard rose in little puffs as people walked around on it.

"Mister, where do you want the bandstand?" A workman with dungarees and a cap worn backward called. "It needs to be away from the house, because those stucco walls are gonna bounce the sound."

"What sound? Wait, what are you doing?"

"A sound system? I'm sure there's something in the CC&R's says you can't have a sound system." Tan bathrobe did an anxious little dance. The dry dust puffed around his feet.

"Look, I was in bed and I got up to see what in hell all this noise was--"

"It's fucking 8 A.M!"

"There's no reason to be upset," Diesel lowered his hands, palms down. "I'll have this straightened out. Wait a minute," he swiveled, "who are you?"

"Cake," grunted one of two men carrying a huge white box. "Needs refrigeration. Gonna be too hot today. I had to leave my truck inside your garage wall; it's the only shade. You know you got no trees?"

"You've taken up all the street parking." A woman in a white tennis outfit strode up the driveway. "I mean, it's really inconsiderate. Come look. Come here and see for yourself."

"Get that out of here!" Diesel waved his hands at the men with the box. "What are you talking about, a cake."

"Can't take it out, Mister. Can't run around with a cake, this weather."

There was a loud crash from the driveway.

"Look what you done to my truck!" one of the cake men yelled from behind the box.

"That was a stupid place to leave it." The bandstand guy ran back, "Nobody can see it around that wall."

"I can't help it if this guy can't decide where to put the cake. I'm gonna have to call my boss about the truck. Mister, you got to tell us where to put this."

"No, no, wait. I want to speak to your boss." Diesel said.

A man in a khaki outfit with Dryweather Gardens stitched on the shirt came across the yard. "Mister Diesel, I think we better put in a deck for the ceremony; you need to sign for the extra charge. I brought up all the turf you ordered, but nobody told me your yard's all cut up, and I can't guarantee to keep down the dust--"

"I did not order turf. I have a detailed plan for this garden; it does not include turf--"

"Sure, Mister, you need it. Otherwise it's going to look like hell for the wedding." Dryweather Gardens said. "Hey Sam," he bellowed, "back up the truck and start unrolling that turf--"

"No!" yelled the cake guy. "No, my truck is--"

There was another loud crash from the driveway, this time with breaking glass.

"No!" yelled the cake guy. "No, no, what, everybody here is crazy?"

"Who the hell left a truck behind the garage wall where you can't see it?" Another man with Dryweather Gardens on his shirt came running up the drive.

"I want to know right now what you're going to do about all these trucks blocking the street," the tennis lady pointed. "I'm not having my friends park half a mile away when they come for a game today. I'm just not having it."

"Lady, go home." Diesel's arms were windmilling.

"I'm the president of the Homeowners' Association, and we'll see what the police say." She strode away, shorts snapping.

"She's the president of the Homeowners' Association?" Diesel asked.

"Yeah, she's a real ball buster," said tan bathrobe. "Hey, maybe she can get them to tow that truck blocking my driveway. Barbara," he ran after her, "he's got people blocking my driveway and the maid is double-parked, she can't get in."

"And I'm bringing you up before the City's Board of Architectural Review for the wholesale destruction of your trees." She turned at the end of the drive.

"I didn't cut the trees--"

"Then who did?"

"I don't know--"

"A likely story." Her thin lips curled down. "The board will simply have no credibility if it does not enforce the CC&R's."

"Blocking the driveway; it's a fire hazard," tan bathrobe said. "I have a lawyer to handle this--"

"So sue me." Diesel snapped. "I'm a lawyer."

"For Christ's sake," the cake guy said, "I'm still holding this thing and now my truck's been hit twice."

A slender young man with a blond ponytail came up the drive, wearing a white chef's jacket, black and white checkered pants, and leather clogs.

"Honeydew." He said.

"What?"

"Honeydew Healthful Caterers. You've got to tell somebody to pull out so I can pull in and unload the tables."

"Go away."

"I do not know who's in charge here, but there are two men screaming, absolutely screaming at each other about their trucks, and I'm afraid there's going to be violence."

"I said go away."

"What do you mean, go away? I have fifty tables to unload here."

"No." Diesel moaned.

"Don't clatter those dishes," Honeydew turned to the rising noise behind him, "you'll chip them."

"Well, we can't use the rolling carts," a voice complained, "the yard is all dirt."

"Oh my God," Honeydew put the back of his hand on his forehead, "not another of those awful dirt yards. Don't people realize there's absolutely no way of keeping that dirt out of the food? It flies in the air every time somebody takes a step. We'll have to cover the dishes. It kills the visual effect."

"No." Diesel's head turned from side to side. "This is not happening. Not again."

"And I can tell you, if you don't get me room for my flatbed truck, I'm not unloading. I am not going to have my people carrying fifty tables through some kind of sidewalk brawl."

"You're not carrying any tables--"

"Then you just won't have any party."

"I'm not HAVING A PARTY!"

"Right." Honeydew nodded. "That's it, then. I cannot work in a setup with absolutely no organization. I'm pulling my staff out."

"Good."

"And you'll find my contract calls for payment in full once you have booked a date and guaranteed it with your credit card, which you did. I am not responsible for crazies." He whirled and left.

"Mister, the cake!"

"We blew a circuit hooking up the sound system." A man in a Grateful Dead tee shirt ambled around the corner of the house. "Where's your box?"

"Ernie, where in the goddam hell you been?" The bandstand guy yelled from the foot of the driveway. "Come over here, look at the truck."

"Mister," said the cake guy, "I got to put this down."

"Then put it down."

"Good." They set it on the dirt. "That's $1,975."

"What?"

"C.O.D," said the cake man. "The girl told you when you ordered."

"I didn't order a cake. I didn't order this stuff--"

"Barbara says you're some film guy," tan bathrobe was back.

191

"Film guys?" The cake man's hands did a pushaway. "No wonder. Big shots, big egos, they get high on coke, don't know what the hell they ordered."

"This can't happen." Diesel covered his face. "This is not an accident. Not twice. Somebody is doing this, persecuting me, somebody crazy. It's terrible when you don't know who's hitting you--"

"Yeah, well, I still need the cash."

A van threaded its way between the trucks and a TV cameraman climbed on the roof.

"Mr. Diesel," an attractive young woman shoved a microphone in front of Diesel, "Eyewitness News. May we have your version of this incident?"

"No, no TV cameras." Diesel waved his hands in front of his face, "Where did you come from?"

"I called them." The tennis lady strode up behind the TV lady. "I want a public record of this outrage. People move into a seven-figure neighborhood and destroy it this way!"

"Who's doing this?" Diesel roared. He repeated just the one word. "Who?"

A large truck parked perpendicular to the back of the TV van. "Flowers," one of the men in the truck sang out.

"These people attacking me have been trained," yelled Diesel. "This is organized. It's terrorists."

"Terrorists? Where?" Tan bathrobe yelped.

"The Rolls," Diesel's arms were flailing. "I see it now. That's exactly what they'd attack; they see it as a mark of affluence."

"I'm getting out of here," Tan bathrobe turned and started running, holding the front of his bathrobe together. "I'm going home."

"They're trying to break me; they're toying with me."

Tan bathrobe crashed into the cake men. "Let me out of here, you morons," he bellowed. "Terrorists. They may bomb this guy."

"A bomb? Where?" The TV lady leaped across Diesel and shoved the microphone at tan bathrobe.

"Mandy, that went out over the air," the man on top of the TV van waved a cutting motion, "Jesus, you'll have every nut in Southern California driving up here with the wife and kids--"

"That ends our interview," the TV lady smiled into the camera. "Back to the studio."

"There's no way to know who's doing this--" Diesel said.

"Are you okay?" the TV lady came back. "You've gone white."

"Dead white," the cameraman put on his shoulder rig and focused on Diesel.

"Who says you're a TV crew; it could be you--" Diesel grabbed the TV lady.

"Let go of me," she squealed, "you're making marks on my arm."

"This guy, Diesel, is flipping out and he's got Mandy," the cameraman spoke into a walkie talkie.

"Mandy, they've got us boxed in." the TV driver called, looking behind the van.

"What do you mean, boxed in?" the TV lady said. "Get me out!"

"My God, we're trapped." Tan bathrobe extricated himself from the cake and ran down the drive, his steps punctuated by his flapping bathrobe belt.

"Get me out right fucking now." The TV lady screamed.

"We can't move," the cameraman said. "Look," he pointed.

Moving in regal formation and taking the entire street, two abreast, gleaming in the early morning sun, was a fleet of eight matching black stretch limos.

Chapter Twenty Six

Visitors touring Hollywood, California, are disappointed to find it resembles a set for Miami Vice. Back in the 60's there were hopes that some of the art deco buildings could be saved, at least some of the movie palaces along Hollywood Boulevard, with their garish colors and startling Mayan and Egyptian facades. But a new type of cartoon architecture triumphed: golden arches, fake tile-roofed burrito stands, revolving chicken buckets that filled the street with a pervading odor of grease. Then the drug dealers started contributing to the curbside supply of paper wrappers.

At this hour of an early Sunday afternoon the street looked sleepy, but Avery Ford knew from experience that in every alley and vacant building people were shooting up. He stood at the outside magazine stand that ran fifty feet along the side of a brick building and closed with an accordion gate on the boulevard side. Best damn magazine stand in Los Angeles, but you had to watch the nabe.

He bought the Sunday **New York Times**, **Theater Arts**, **People** Magazine, and the **Recycler Auto News**; then withdrew to Musso and Frank's, walking through the restaurant, waving to a few people, stopping to talk to an actor he knew who was directing a play in a storefront north of Franklin Avenue. Guy said he had a role Ford could read for. No pay, of course. Just a chance to be seen—you never knew who'd show up in the audience. Ford always went to the back room at Musso and Frank's, even though he had to tip the waiter more. At least he could spread out the papers.

"Where you been lately?" the rheumy-eyed waiter asked. He looked like the building had been built around him fifty years before. "We used to see a lot more of you."

"I'm out in Burbank on a western," Ford said, sliding behind the table of a booth on the side, so he could spread out the papers on the tan Formica® tabletop. "How's the grilled liver?"

"Good, same as always. Be a while, they're just lighting the grill. Takes a half hour after they light it."

194

"Fine," Ford said, "no sweat. Bring me a salad, dressing on the side." The waiter brought a place setting.

"Rudy, you're looking good. I been coming here twenty years, and you were gray when I started. How old are you?"

"Mind your own business," the waiter said. "I'll get the salad."

"Tell them no salt--" Ford stopped. The article, on page 89 of the April 4ᵗʰ **People** Magazine, was headlined: "Finding a Malvina Hoffman Original Gives Town Champagne Ending." A photo of the plaza in Plonktown occupied the top two-thirds of the page, with townspeople in front of the statue hugging each other and drinking champagne.

"The restored statue of Josiah Plonk is sitting in its plaza after providing a major surprise--" the article began. Avery Ford did not read the rest of the text. His attention was on the full length photo of the statue. He could see the head and the hand. And the foot.

He stared at the photo, then lifted the magazine so he could see it better in the light from the doorway. Then he hugged himself and whooped. Nobody at Musso and Frank's so much as raised an eye from a plate of eggs. Ford picked up the magazine and ran out the rear door to the parking lot.

The waiter shuffled over carrying the salad and looked at the newspapers strewn around the table and at Ford's back retreating out the door.

"Meshuganah. We really get 'em in this place." He shrugged. "Didn't I first tell him the liver would be a while?"

Chapter Twenty Seven

"No, I do not know what's on Ford's mind." Zoltan Diesel propped hand-tooled cowboy boots on the railing of his deck. "But he has been a major nuisance, constantly nagging me for more marketing on the Plonktown pilot. The man is unstable."

"Maybe he's on to some kind of work," Herb Boland said. "Maybe with something for me."

"Let's just hope he hasn't fallen off the wagon. My life has been sufficiently weird without that." Diesel ran fingers through hair that needed cutting and now formed a wispy doughnut around his bald spot.

"Avery's really been pushing for work; he could have come up with something. I need to work."

"And, Herb, I do not need to hear your theory about a Northwest Indian curse again."

"I could use extra work, get after my bills--"

"Because this has nothing to do with any goddam Indian curse; it's a vindictive scheme, a deliberate blind attack, and I will find out who."

"Every morning I get all these pay or die letters. It's depressing. I think it's starting to affect my work. I used to get all these ideas—wake up in the middle of the night with great ideas, I'd write them down. Now I wake up, all I think about is bills."

"Ford's contract requires him to stay sober until the western is finished. I intend to enforce that."

"He's been sober."

"You look terrible." Diesel looked at Boland. Boland's foot was in a cast which was now dirty gray and which pushed up one side of his baggy sweat pants. The sweat pants were stained, as was his tee shirt. "And frankly, Herb, I wouldn't work with you again without a specific clause about drinking. I'm going to make some coffee; I want you sober to deal with whatever nonsense Avery comes up with. Diesel poured coffee beans in a bean blaster marked "Braun®" and whirred the motor.

"It's for the pain." Boland propped his foot cast on the railing. "Lemme tell you how long it takes a broken toe to heal. It's weeks, and every time you step on it--"

"There are other physical conditions that take a long time, that change peoples lives, but people don't drink. Personal conditions people don't talk about."

"There's Ford."

The red MG glided inside the gate and Ford parked, then leaped over the side door and waved to them. He carried packages.

"Well, we know his coordination's good," Boland observed.

Diesel removed a streamlined coffeemaker, also marked "Braun®," from the wet bar. He filled the glass pot with water and plugged it in.

"Gentlemen," Ford brandished two brown paper bags, "wine for my friends, two leaders in the communications field. Glasses, uh—vidrios, andale, muchacho."

The houseboy looked at Ford blankly.

"He's from Taiwan." Diesel said. "What is this?"

"The finest of jug wine," Ford revolved the bottles, using both hands, displaying the label like a sommelier, "We're celebrating."

"Do you mind telling me what?" Boland tried to scratch inside the cast on his foot with a pencil.

"Why, knowledge, Herb, knowledge is always cause for celebration, and I'm about to lay some vital knowledge on you two."

"This is why you telephoned and insisted we meet you immediately? Are you drunk?" Diesel demanded.

"Certainly not," Ford said with dignity. "If I was drunk, I would miss this, and I wouldn't want to miss this. In fact, Zoltan, I drove all the way up here because I wanted to be sure I was the first to tell you. That's important to me."

"All right, Avery, you've finally got center stage. So get on with it." Diesel flicked a glance at him.

"Ah, what an evening, what a view of the gardens— Zoltan, I can't see clearly in this light, is that bamboo?"

"Don't start," Diesel snapped. "Have you any idea what it's going to cost to uproot that stuff? You can't just pull out bamboo, you know. It goes way down. You have to dig down about ten feet and then re-sod the whole garden. I tell you, it's like a biblical plague--"

"Or an Indian curse."

"Are you starting that again?" Diesel roared at Boland.

Ford raised his arms over the bamboo, his voice took on a Charlton Heston resonance, "and the servant said to the owner of the fields, 'sir, did you not plant good seed? How then are there weeds?' and the owner said, 'an enemy hath done this.' Ah, the glasses. You'll excuse me if I don't partake. Can I have a coffee?"

"The gardener's a total incompetent. I personally supervised this planting, so the seed he used had to be contaminated."

"At least you've got money." Boland lifted his head. "I put earnest money down on a house in Venice and now I'm going to lose my deposit because everybody thinks I'm a deadbeat."

"This time I really can explain it." Ford said.

"Oh Christ, not again," said Boland.

"The bamboo is small," said Diesel. "I'm looking into ripping it out before it takes over the other shrubs, whatever that requires."

"And all the landlords have this service where they register you if you've ever been evicted in California," Boland said, "and I got evicted because two rent checks bounced, so now I've lost my apartment and nobody'll rent to me."

"The alternative is weed killer. It'll kill everything, and the gardener says he's not sure if even that will get the bamboo, because we've been fertilizing so heavily." Diesel poured the coffee in spurts, as if he couldn't manage a steady stream. Some of it splashed over the rim of one of the cups.

"It's just bad luck, rotten luck." Boland drank the glass of red wine in three swallows. "Who figured the computer would foul up? I thought the money on the statements I got was in my account. Well, naturally. But in this town, you bounce one check, they forget what you've done for ten years, they forget a living room full of awards--"

"Ah, Herb," Ford danced over to Boland, "the last award in your living room was this one." Ford handed Boland the photo in **People** and pointed to the head of the statue.

"What is it?" Boland tried to focus. "Hey, this is Stacy's head, the head was in my living room." He abruptly sat straight up. "Avery, where'd you get this?"

"And you, Zoltan, you might remember this foot. And the hand." Ford plucked the magazine from Boland, who clutched for it, and passed it to Diesel.

Diesel looked at the photo and then at the two and a half- acre bamboo thicket stretching across his property, slow comprehension draining his face.

"See, Zoltan, knowledge. I may be a former drunk, but I can still enlighten you."

"You—you had something to do with this?" Diesel lunged for Ford.

"Lighten up, Zoltan," Ford ducked behind the wet bar. "I couldn't have pulled this off. Admire it, maybe."

"You damn hack--"

"You remember those poor slobs up north, the ones redid their whole town for our pilot film?" Ford came out the other side of the wet bar. "Lumbermen, weren't they, didn't know from legal."

"Plonktown?" Boland grabbed back the magazine. "Plonktown did this?"

"All they know about is trees. Oh, and bamboo, of course. And the gas station guy, the one the crew used his electricity and stiffed him? I think he knows about Rollses. You still with me, Zoltan?" Ford retained a hand on the wet bar.

Diesel seemed to have a problem breathing. "A bunch of yokels up north did this? To me? A bunch of these bastards schemed—can you imagine anything more deceitful--"

"Well, I wouldn't call them schemes," Ford tilted his head judiciously. "Acts of retribution, maybe."

Diesel looked around him as if to fend off an attack. "The financing reschedule on that pilot was a business matter; it was nothing personal."

"I think they took it personally, Zoltan. Now, I wanted to be the one to tell you that, since you got me cheap by telling everyone in the biz I was in Alcoholics Anonymous and my drinking was affecting my career."

"What career? You're a hack actor. You won't ever be more than a hack actor." Diesel spat.

"Exactly," Ford nodded. "That's why I rushed over. Us hacks have to learn to grab our moments."

"You smirking bastard, you're laughing are you, you think you had trouble getting work before--"

"Of course," Ford executed a graceful side step to avoid Diesel, "I stopped on the way, called Sid Brothers on the **Times**. He's real curious what was going on with that TV thing you did up here at the house Sunday morning, Zoltan, says he understands they got footage of you attacking a woman TV reporter, and you squashed it. I told him I might meet him, fill him in."

"Sid Brothers is going to cover it?" Boland said. "Hey, that's not bad PR. Maybe we should pick up on it. To market the pilot."

"Herb, I don't yet know why justice came to you in the form of fouled up computer statements."

"Avery," Boland picked up his foot with both hands and dropped it on the deck. He winced. "You're telling me I'm being punished for what we did in Plonktown by some kind of computer poltergeist? I think you've got the d.t.'s."

Boland turned to Diesel. "I didn't want Avery on the Plonktown pilot. I fought for the guy I wanted in the role, the guy I knew could do it. You put Avery on me because he was cheap."

"Thank you, Herb," Ford said. "And in return for that gracious remark, I'm going to tell you something. I'll bet if we looked, we could find somebody up there among the dripping redwoods knows as much about computers as the gas station guy does about Rollses."

200

"Why me?" Boland's voice was wounded. "Remember, I'm the one argued against Zoltan screwing those people. All I want is a chance to work--"

"Oh, you were fine when you thought you were getting a bonus for bringing in the pilot at budget," Diesel's mouth worked as if he couldn't swallow. "We stopped hearing about that goddam town then, didn't we."

"Gentlemen, gentlemen, time goes fast when you're having fun," Ford said. "Drink up."

"Pay them, so we'll pay them, a small payment, get them off me," Diesel said. "Say, ten per cent--"

"Zoltan, we owe a total up there of about $500,000," Boland said, "including the money to the city."

"$500,000?" Diesel said. "That's typical of you, Herb, immature. You're great as long as everything is going your way. One thing goes wrong, you fold. We need to negotiate--" Diesel took a large swallow out of the glass of red wine. He spluttered, choked, and spilled wine down one leg of his fawn colored pants. "My God," he gasped, when he could speak. "What is that crap?"

"Why cheap red wine," Ford displayed the label. "You know. Plonk."

"That's your idea of a great pun?" Diesel slapped down his glass, which fell over the railing into the bamboo.

"Just a minute," Boland's eyes were on the horizon and his hand was moving horizontally over the railing, fingers moving; he was mentally typing. "Everybody shut up."

"You realize there is no way this is a normal reaction to what was an accounting matter," Diesel said. "These people are paranoid, maybe even violent. Which is why it's better to pay them a small plink. I'll bet there's all kinds of inbreeding in that town up there; these are crazies--"

"You know what we've got here." Boland's voice had a hard excitement which made Ford quietly put his coffee on the wet bar. "We've got the perfect series pilot."

"What's the perfect series pilot?" Diesel stepped around a puddle of spilled wine and sat down.

"Zoltan, listen, it's a natural, it would write itself. A new series about Plonktown. All we have to do is follow what happened, one segment for each thing they did, say a story arc of six shows."

"We've got free advance publicity; that statue is all over the magazines, and I mean the nationals, not locals." Avery Ford's voice was excited and he left the protection of the wet bar.

"Think of the visuals! That statue up in Plonktown, a long opening shot of the plaza, sort of the theme. And the mountains and bay, Northern California as a locale." Boland pulled a small note pad from the pocket of his sweats and pulled the cap off a pen with his mouth.

"You think I'm going to let you make this public, with me as the butt?" Diesel's voice rose.

"Zoltan, we'll take it verbatim--"

"What are you doing? Are you writing down what I'm saying? Stop that!" Diesel stood up, arms windmilling, and knocked over the coffee into his crotch. A brown stain formed on the other pants leg from the wine stain.

"Come on, Zoltan, I'm a professional writer, anything said in front of me is fair game unless I say it isn't and I didn't." Boland propped the note pad on the railing and scribbled frantically.

"This is the worst sort of betrayal--"

"Hey, betrayal. All writing is a betrayal. People tell you things; they think you're listening and they open their guts to you, and you run home and write it in a story. You still wanna be a writer? All writers are cannibals, anybody doesn't know that doesn't know us."

"The money. Where do you think you're going to get the money?" Diesel stabbed a finger at Boland. "Remember the money? You said yourself, nobody in the biz will touch you right now--"

"From you, Zoltan."

"Your fingers will rot off on your goddam keyboard first--"

"I don't figure you've got much choice, Zoltan." Boland tilted his head. "If you produce it, everybody'll say, 'Well, it can't really be about him.' But if somebody else produces it; with all the publicity--"

"No! Now I said no--"

"Zoltan, for two years I've been listening to you yap about being creative, about you're gonna do some writing. Now's it." Boland juggled the pen and licked the point. "This is going to be the funniest thing on the tube. You're going to be the toast of Hollywood."

"Plus we get into the national papers with this statue story." Ford said.

"Right. Maybe we could do something with this sculptress, this—what's her name in the magazine, Malvina Hoffman. Hey, is she still around? Avery, get on the phone to the library--" Boland clunked on his cast toward the doors to Diesel's den. "Not Plonktown." he said. "Another library."

"We could have the debut party for the film in the plaza up in Plonktown." Ford was dancing rapidly on the deck, "The reporters would love it, a free trip."

"Herb, listen," Diesel grabbed Boland's arm. "They screwed you, these people. These bastards up there somehow screwed up your statements. Would it be too much to remind you they deliberately ruined you?"

"So what?" Boland seemed surprised. "Zoltan, you don't understand, we've got a really hot idea here."

"How can you roll over like this?" Diesel screamed. "They attacked me physically--"

"They attacked you physically?" Boland came back. "Who?"

"I don't want to talk about it."

"You still don't get it, Zoltan. We're going to work this idea. It's going to make phenomenal TV. That's what you do when you create, you see it's beautiful and you run with an idea."

"Herb, we could still do it, you know," Ford ran to Boland, elbows pumping. "Even if Zoltan doesn't want to do it. We have a great idea and all this fantastic publicity. Lots of people will want this series."

"No!" Diesel said.

"No, what?"

"No, uh, no, don't be hasty." Diesel's hands groped for the back of the chair. "I haven't said I wouldn't do it. I am nothing if not open to a good project--" Diesel seemed to be strangling.

"In fact," Ford reached Boland, "We'll do better putting it out for a bid. Zoltan's got sort of a sleazy rep."

"You don't have to do that," Diesel said. "I can see the value in the idea, something really creative to work on."

"Zoltan, you'd get a nosebleed if you really had to create something," Boland said. "All you know is how to juggle figures to screw people."

"Now Herb, Avery--"

"Listen, Zoltan, I need to use your word processor—I need to get some ideas down quick, because they're coming too fast now for a pencil and I don't want to lose any." Boland's voice lost its slurred tone. His body changed its habitual forward slump and he stopped favoring his foot.

He opened the French doors of Diesel's study. "And I'm doing the budget this time, Zoltan. No more cheapies. Remember, I'm writing your role."

"You want to pay those scheming plotting pricks--"

"Herb, listen," Avery stepped between Boland and Diesel. "You're right, I can always sense these things. This could be really hot, there's not another thing like it on the tube. The thing is, you know I'm available to play myself--"

"We'll have to get the people in Plonktown to sign off the rights--" Boland turned back.

"Who better to play me than me, right?" Ford said.

"We'd have to pay them what we owe them. I'll give them a call. I left there on pretty good terms with them. Well, with some of them. But I think it's doable if we use their town in the new series--"

"And I'm a natural to play myself," Avery finished.

"And then we'd have to pay them in advance for the new show, of course."

"Even if you write me as a drunk," Ford urged. "I do a great drunk, Herb. Lots of practice."

"Pay in advance, have you lost your mind--" Diesel was holding on to the back of the chair, his body sagging.

"Well, otherwise they won't do it. Be reasonable." Boland headed into the study. He turned.

"And we're going back to Plonktown."